Scraps of Laughter

I0668113

for Ladies

Sandra Waggoner

Wagon Tracks
PUBLISHING

The page is my canvas.

Family and friends gifted and spilled the paint.

They threw off their shoes and danced in a wild frenzy.

Their footsteps painted my page.

And me? I sprinkled the glitter!

Thank you, Family and Friends!

P.S. Thanks for the Laughter!

"A merry heart doeth good like a medicine: but a broken spirit drieth the bones."

Proverbs 17:22

TABLE OF CONTENTS

Scraps of Laughter
for Ladies

The Terrible Red Truck

I pressed my nose against the window and watched the truck clamber past, leaving dust clouds behind. Excitement surged within me. For two days, we'd been dumping the wheat in a growing pile on the ground while watching the skies. My harvest job was truck driver. Every year, I would load up my kids and bring them to harvest because I wanted them to taste what growing up on a farm was like. Memories flooded me, and I craved them for my children. It worked. They were as excited as me! But with the first load to the elevator, the old green truck died. The temperature gauge sped higher than the miles-per-hour gauge ever had. Daddy had coaxed the old green truck to the shed and dumped it, and there it rested in peace. There was no time to fix it. The wheat had to be cut now. So, the piles had begun. Then, a neighbor heard of our plight and sent us a spare that he had.

I turned from the window. Clay was the only close kid, and I burst forth with the news, "The truck is here! The truck is here!"

"Yahoo!" Clay jumped up and twirled, letting his Batman cape fly. "We get to go to the elevator!"

"Yep. We sure do," I swung him in the air.

As he came down for a landing, he looked me in the eye, "Just you and me, yeah!"

"Yep. The girls miss out this time." They had spent the night at a girl cousin's, Htebazile's, Ardnassac's, and Aassilla's. That is their names spelled backwards. Clay had felt left out but now he would get even. He got to go on the first harvest trip to

9

the elevator!

I turned to the window again. The auger was chugging, and my uncle and dad were scooping. "Let's get ready, Clay. It won't take them long."

Together, we trudged down the farm road, dust puffs igniting with each step. Clay chased yellow butterflies across the alfalfa. By the time we made it to the truck, it was loaded and ready to go. Dad was climbing the steps up the combine. I ran to stop him, "Dad!"

He turned halfway up the ladder, "Yeah?"

"Dad, you have to show me how to drive this truck," I waved toward the thing.

Some glimmer, maybe humor, sparked his eyes. He nodded, "Have Uncle Lawrence show ya; I gotta cut."

He'd been by the truck. Clay was there now, but not Uncle Lawrence. I scanned the scene and yelled, "Wait!" He was stepping into the other combine and would be gone within seconds. I ran and grabbed the combine rail to anchor this machine. "Wait!"

Uncle Lawrence stopped.

"Dad told me to ask you to show me how to drive that truck," I explained.

Uncle Lawrence looked at the haze of wheat chaff marking Dad's distant combine, nodded, and climbed back down the ladder. Together, we approached the truck. He yanked on the door handle several times before the ominous thing cranked open. The truck's floor came to my chin, so Uncle Lawrence began instruction there. He was a man of few words. He pointed. "Here's the clutch." It was the closest. "Here's the brake." Then he paused but didn't look at me. I think he wanted to discourage questions.

Scraps of Laughter for Ladies

"There's the gas pedal."

My eyes popped wide. There was no pedal. There was a black rod shoved through the rested floorboard. Quickly, Uncle Lawrence continued his lesson. "There's the stick shift, there's the steering wheel, and the keys are in the ignition." He turned to go but stopped to remind me, "Be sure ya take the truck out of gear to raise the bed, and," he paused, "if ya need any help, they can help ya at the elevator." Uncle Lawrence left.

Clay was already in the truck and bouncing. Nothing was left to do but climb up the truck ladder and go.

I sat on the hot seat…or in the hot seat and found I was too far away to reach the pedals and the gas rod. I dug beside and beneath the seat to feel for the adjusting lever. It wouldn't budge. Next, I dug out an ancient, quilted flannel jacket that smelled like mice. I wadded it up and wedged it behind me. That helped.

With a deep breath, I pressed the clutch and switched the key. That motor roared, vibrating the whole county!

"Varoom!" Clay shouted.

I closed my eyes and prayed.

Again and again, I yanked the gearshift hoping for first. Finally! I pressed the gas rod, and that truck bucked like a bull from the chute! Clay was whammed back against the seat, but his smile only grew bigger. All the way down the farm road, that truck was a bump magnet. I prayed for the eight-second buzzer, but whoever was the timekeeper wasn't on duty!

As we turned onto the main country road, I had

my first battle with the turning of that truck. I gripped and struggled with the steering wheel. "Listen, Truck; you are newer than my old green truck, so you should drive easier!" I told it. I won. That truck turned. On the country road, that truck shifted pretty good, and I felt a smile twinging. Harvest breeze fingered my hair. Clay's Batman cape soared behind him as he stuck his head out the window. This was great.

Turn #1: I pushed the brakes to slow and downshift. No brakes. I scanned the dashboard. I knew our neighbor had said that it had air brakes. Maybe there was a button you pushed when you wanted to use the brakes. Nothing. I yanked my foot off the gas rod and began stomping the brakes. With the irrigation ditch looming before us, the brakes kicked in. Dust from behind overtook us. Clay blinked, "Why did we stop here? The elevator's that way!"

I nodded. Reverse? It was marked on the gear shift knob, but I still had to slam it around a few times before it went into gear.

With a lurch, we took out again. The only turn now was into the elevator, and thankfully, it was a gradual obtuse turn, and we made it fine.

I surveyed the scene. "Yes!" There was no one in front of us! I drove straight to the scales...on the scales…and...off the scales. That stupid truck wouldn't stop!

Clay giggled, "Look!" With waving arms, an elevator man ran to catch up with us.

"Wait!" he yelled. "We have to weigh you first!"

I didn't even try to explain. I just nodded and fought with the reverse again. When we lurched into reverse, I hoped the elevator man was out of the way!

Scraps of Laughter
for Ladies

They weighed us and motioned us to the dump pit. We snail-paced it there because I knew these brakes and reverse now. They had Alzheimer's. The elevator dump man motioned me to stop. I did! Then he motioned our truck to dump. I remembered to take it out of gear first, then pull the lift knob. I pulled the lift knob then I yanked the lift knob. "This stupid truck!" I ground through gritted teeth. With one foot for security on the brakes that didn't work, I wedged the other foot into the dashboard and began pulling the lift knob. Nothing.

"Mom, the elevator guy wants us to dump," Clay told me.

I glanced in the rearview mirror. Yep. He was motioning "up" alright. I recognized that gesture. I gripped the knob and tried again.

The elevator man rolled his eyes with a "woman driver" look and moseyed to my door. My foot was still plastered on the dashboard. Clumsily, I dropped my leg, kicking the dashboard knobs. The windshield wipers shot into action.

"Great!" I staccatoed my words. "This truck has no brakes, no power steering, hardly a reverse but the windshield wipers work!"

"Why'd ya turn on the wipers, Mom? It ain't raining," Clay asked.

The elevator man tapped on my door.

"Listen," I poured out my story. "This is a borrowed truck. I can't seem to get the bed to rise. Could you help me?"

"Up, si', Senora, up," he said.

"Mom," Clay whispered, "he don't talk English."

I groaned. The elevator man walked to the back

13

of the truck, still motioning the up signal.

Again, I positioned myself; one foot on the brake, one foot on the dashboard, hands on the lift knob, and teeth ground together. Finally! That truck groaned and began the slow, cranky journey up.

"Yea!" Clay applauded.

Grain dust choked through the elevator tunnel and silted through our windows. Clay pulled his Batman cape over his nose. I watched the rearview mirror for the signal to drop the bed. It came. I thrust the knob clear to the dashboard. That truck bed griped halfway down and stopped. I didn't care. Grain trucks can be driven that way! With clutch underfoot and gear shift in hand, the wrestling match began. I couldn't conquer first gear, but with an empty truck, you can start out in second gear if you give it enough gas. I eased out the clutch and smashed the gas rod.

We tore out of the elevator tunnel, whapping Clay to the floor. "Wow!" He shouted, "This baby's got power!"

I put a Full Nelson on the steering wheel to turn that "Baby," and we wheeled about and headed for the scales at full speed. Then, I remembered the brakes. I yanked my foot from the gas rod and wildly pumped the brakes. It happened. Two inches from the end of the scales, I killed that truck. Clay was on the floor again. Slowly, he climbed back onto the seat rubbing his elbow. "Need a band-aid?" I asked.

Clay nodded.

"When we get home," I promised.

Clay slid to the door and took up a good grip on the window sill.

"Here's your ticket and a pop for the little one," the elevator man smiled.

14

Scraps of Laughter
for Ladies

"Thanks."

"Your Dad get a new truck?" he asked.

"Just borrowed. His broke down," I explained.

He nodded. "Ya know the bed's still up?"

I chuckled. "Yep. Thought the breeze on the way home might clean it out."

"Mmm. Your wipers?" he wanted to know.

I liked my lips. "Clay, my son here, is learning to count." I lied.

Clay glared.

He nodded again and tapped the bill of his cap. "Well, have a good one!" He backed away from the truck.

"Clay," I ordered, "don't open that root beer yet. Wait until we get home."

I pushed the clutch, found second gear, and smashed the gas rod. We took off. Clay's knuckles were white as he clung to the window ledge with one hand and the pop can with the other. We were doing a pretty good lick down the road when that truck blasted and belched forth a sonic boom! That truck bed collapsed! My heart stopped. Clay dove to the floor and covered his head with his Batman cape.

It was then I decided to take the shortcut, the one over the ditch and caddy-cornered across a bordered field. That truck didn't have shocks, either. We were catapulted like popcorn in that cab. As we neared a place somewhere in the middle of the field, I began jamming the brakes. I killed it...dead.

Dusty silence settled. Clay peeked from beneath his Batman cape, "Are we safe?"

Safe? Maybe. There had been a few close calls. "I think so, Honey."

His eyes flashed from side to side before he left

his refuge and found a more secure one in my arms. We dropped out of that truck. I noticed his Root beer can. Five fingerprints were embedded in the aluminum.

"Ya gonna tell Grampa about the truck?" Clay asked.

I looked at the combine across the field. "No." I didn't want any questions.

My legs shook as we trudged across the stubble. I pulled out my phone, dialed my husband, and poured out my battle story ending with, "Just where is some kind of knob that works those air brakes?"

"Well, Hon, what kind of truck is it?" he asked.

"Red! It is horrible red!"

Silence sounded through the line. "Tell you what. I'll be right there, Hon."

I hoped it would be before the next trip to the elevator.

It was.

First, he eyed the old plaid coat and asked, "Why didn't you adjust the seat?" He yanked the lever, and the seat scooted forward. "Let's take this baby for a spin around the section." He slapped the gearshift into first, and off we went. With the first pull of the steering wheel, he stated, "Needs power steering fluid." When he tried the brakes, he said. "Mmm, the line must have come loose. We'll have this baby running like new in no time!"

And he did.

But to me, 'This Baby,' would forever be That Terrible Red Truck!

Scraps of Laughter
for Ladies

Jr. Camp

The first week after school was out, we rented the campground at Hidden Falls Ranch for Jr. Camp. Several of the churches would come together, so we usually had at least one hundred campers. Greg was in charge of the camp, so I guess that made him a director. I got to be the camp cook. My sister, Cathy, was my helper, so, yeah! It was a week of visiting, laughter, and fun!

Our helpers slash counselors ended up being our older kids. We needed enough to have one counselor in each bunkhouse. We only had Boone and Tandolynn, plus a couple of my sister's girls who were old enough to take charge of juniors. But we needed another couple of guys. Boone had a wrestling buddy who had been coming to church with him. He was a newborn Christian and had never been to a Jr. Camp before. He was called Duck, and this was going to be great!

Sunday night, after the lights were out, Duck slipped into the dining hall where Cathy and I were going over the menu for Monday. Greg was munching on cookies.

"Bro. Greg," Duck asked, "these boys are driving me crazy. Just what are my duties anyway?"

"Did you leave those kids alone in the cabin in the night?" I asked, a bit worried.

"Naw, Boone said he could watch both cabins, but I don't know what to do," Duck said.

Greg smiled, "Well, Duck, it is kind of like baby-sitting. You have to make them go to bed. You have to make sure they get up and get dressed and

17

come to the meals on time. During rest periods, you have to make them lie down and keep quiet. If they have questions, you answer them. Stuff like that."

Duck squinted, "Do I have to get up in the night and take them to the bathroom? Derwood wanted me to go with him." Duck paused, "Who would name a kid Derwood anyway?"

I laughed, "Who would name a kid Duck?"

Duck shrugged and laughed. "It's a nickname for Donald. Duck for short. Anyway, Derwood says he's afraid of the dark. I told him to get over it." Duck pulled out a chair, sat down, and grabbed a cookie.

I smiled. "Duck, you are probably going to have to take Derwood to the bathroom because it is dark out here on the rim of the canyon, and there are wild animals roaming the night. Those wild animals live here. Besides, if you don't take him, Duck, he might wet the bed."

Duck groaned, "Oh, no!" He jumped up, skidding the chair across the floor.

"Duck, did you already tell him he had to go outside alone among the wild coyotes?" Greg asked.

"Worse than that," he called over his shoulder from the door, "I told him to go to sleep in my bunk with Boone's bullwhip to keep him safe. I got to get back before he wets my sleeping bag!"

And Duck was gone!

Early the next morning, Cathy was stirring the gravy, and I was getting ready to pull out the biscuits. Duck and Boone barged in the back kitchen door.

"Morning, Duck. Morning, Son. How goes the counseling job?" I asked.

Duck spread his hands, "Mrs. Sandy, I don't remember ever doing the things these boys do."

18

Scraps of Laughter
for Ladies

"Boone slapped him on the back, "You don't have to remember them 'cause you still do them."

Everyone laughed.

"How many trips to the bathroom did you make last night, and was your sleeping bag dry when you got back to your cabin?" I asked.

"Trips through the moonlight? I'm not sure. I think there were about four trips, but I got smart. Now, every time someone wakes me up, I make them all pile out of bed and head to the head. That ought to cut down on the night runs. And as for my sleeping bag? After I yanked Derwood out of it, I decided not to chance anything. I dropped it on the floor. Derwood's job this morning is to bring it over here to see if you would wash it."

Boone chuckled, "Yeah, I watched him dragging it across the cactus and yuccas. It ought to be nice and cozy for you tonight."

"Ahhh, man!" Duck groaned.

"Are all your boys up, dressed, and ready for breakfast?" I asked.

"My boys are already in line for breakfast. I don't mess around," Boone informed all.

"For the most part, I think they are ready," Duck paused. "You know I saw the weirdest thing. I think these boys have no brains. They are all goofballs."

"What did they do, Duck?" Greg had just walked into the kitchen.

Duck slipped his cap off his head and rubbed his other hand through his hair, "I made them get up and head to the bathroom to wash their faces and brush their teeth. We all went. There are five sinks. I took the first sink, and they all lined up beside me. Michael was

19

next to me. I watched him brush his teeth, and then he handed his toothbrush to Lalo. Lalo used the same brush, and then he handed it to Jacob. Jacob used that brush, and then he handed it to Derwood. They all used the very same toothbrush!" Duck was aghast. Then he shrugged, "At least they made Derwood use it last! That kid is something else. But I don't know what they will do tomorrow."

Laughter spread over the room, but Greg warned him, "You might want to put your toothbrush in a safe place."

Duck slapped his hat back on his head, "Oh, I did. They will never find it!"

I pulled my biscuits from the oven and gasped. I took the huge tray and sat it on the butcher block. "Greg, do these biscuits look…"

"Green?" Duck finished the question for me.

"Green, Mom?" Boone laughed.

"What happened?" Greg asked.

"I don't know."

Cathy chuckled, "They are a very pale, nice shade of green."

"Are they safe?" Duck asked the important question.

"They should be," I dragged the next tray out of the oven. Those biscuits were the same color. All five trays were green.

Greg asked, "What are you going to do?"

I spread my hands, "What can I do? I am going to serve them."

"Mom," Boone reasoned, "what if they are poison?"

"They can't be poison. I didn't put anything poison in them," I told everyone in the kitchen. "I just don't want the kids to think something is wrong with them."

There was a pounding at the back door to the kitchen. Greg yanked the heavy door open. There stood Derwood, wreathed in Duck's camo sleeping bag. His pop-bottle eyeglasses pinched the end of his nose, and his new front teeth were so big he didn't seem to be able to close his lips over them. I smiled. I'll bet he missed those baby teeth.

Duck laughed, "Hey, Buddy, drop the bag and come in here. I have a secret mission for you." Duck turned to me and whispered, "I have your guinea pig."

Derwood let the bag fall and tripped over it, trying to get to Duck. "Yes, Sir, Mr. Master Sergeant Duck." Derwood saluted.

I raised my eyebrows, Mr. Master Sergeant Duck?"

Greg laughed and left to ring the breakfast bell.

Derwood was the one who answered, "Mr. Duck is our Master Sergeant."

Duck chuckled, "That's right, Private Derwood. Over here, Private. What color are these biscuits?"

"Green, Sir." He saluted.

"That's right, Private Derwood. Your mission is to spread the word that the biscuits are sprayed with a SECRET UNDER COVER POWER. But first, you need to taste one so you can tell everyone how good they work."

"Yes, Sir. Hey, can I have some jelly, too?" Derwood wanted to know.

"Mrs. Sandy?" Duck asked.

"Sure. Right there on the counter behind you."

Duck grabbed a biscuit and handed it to Derwood. Derwood dipped the spoon into the jelly jar, pulled out a huge jiggling lump, balanced it on top of the biscuit, and shoved the whole thing in his mouth. Crumbs sputtered about his chin, and a hunk of jelly slid down from the corner of his mouth. No one said a word. Derwood chewed a couple of times before he swallowed the wad. We watched his Adam's apple jump up and down several times like a pump handle before his scrawny throat cleared.

"Man, that was good. Can I try another biscuit, Mr. Master Sergeant Duck?" Derwood asked. "I need all the undercover power I can get."

Duck patted his back, "At breakfast. I want you to go out there and spread the word about the SECRET UNDER COVER POWER." Duck stuck his cap back on his head, touched the brim of his hat in a nod, and escorted Derwood out of the kitchen.

"That was fast thinking," I told my sister. "If one child had refused to eat the biscuits, all would have followed suit."

That afternoon, the boys, Boone, and Master Sergeant Duck killed a rattlesnake with every child on the campground watching. They cut the head off and took it out in the boonies to bury it. That night at the campfire, Brother Greg told the story of 'A Snake Without a Rattle.' Every Jr. camper squealed and clamped their hands to their flashlights as if they were glued. We thought the lights would never go out. It was the wee hours of the morning before snores settled in.

Just after breakfast Tuesday morning of camp, Boone and Duck strolled into the kitchen. Boone had been laughing, and it didn't take much to tell it was at Master Sergeant Duck's expense.

Scraps of Laughter
for Ladies

Master Sergeant Duck remembered to yank off his hat before he spoke, "Mrs. Sandy, Boone thought you might have an idea of something really good, a dirty chore I could pull for K. P. on my bunk buddies, all nine of them."

I stopped my mixer, "All nine of them? Why? What did they do?"

Boone slapped Duck's back and hee-hawed, "What didn't they do?"

Master Sergeant Duck's brow furrowed. They found something that looks like kitty litter at the horse barn and filled my sleeping bag. And…under my pillow, they dug up that dead rattlesnake and wound it around a stack of horse apples! Horse apples! I threw my pillow away! But, Mrs. Sandy, I need something gross to give those boys for K.P.! I want to teach them a lesson they won't forget!"

Boone was laughing so hard tears were rolling. I know my son, and I could tell that maybe the whole idea had been his. I was sure Duck would find out later. I wiped my hands on my apron. "Duck, can K.P. wait until after memory verse time?"

He shrugged, "I guess."

"Good. I'll have the brownie batter all done here in a minute. While they are in memory time, you guys can spread the batter on the stalls in the boys' bathroom; then for K. P., you can have the boys clean the bathroom. Will that work?"

"Yuk!" Cathy laughed.

"Sweet!" Duck whistled.

Duck and Boone couldn't wait to get the batter bowls.

Scraps of Laughter for Ladies

Later, they burst through the kitchen doors, almost rolling on the floor. "It was great, Mrs. Sandy. Those boys were gagging," Duck said.

Boone added, "We smeared the brownie mix all over the toilet seats and the stall walls. It looked awful!"

"Yep, and Derwood dropped to the floor in front of the toilet to barf, hit his forehead on the seat, and it chunked his glasses in the water."

"Duck? Did you get his glasses out of the commode for him?" I asked.

"No way! A Sergeant doesn't do what a Private can do. He got them out himself," Duck's eyes were filled with mirth.

"Yeah," Boone added, "he just stuck his hand in the water, fished them out, and shoved them back on his face. They were still dripping water. Derwood said the water inside the stool was cleaner than the stool!"

My sister and I looked at each other, "Has he washed yet?"

"Naw, we'll throw him in the shower later," Duck told us.

"But…" Boone struggled to catch his breath, "The best thing was what Duck did when they were almost done. He leaned against one of the stall doors, took his finger, ran it through a hunk of brownie batter, and made sure all nine boys were watching. Then he stuck his finger in his mouth. Those boys about died! Lalo gagged and said, 'Mr. Duck, I don't think that is good for you!' So, Duck swiped his hand through it and held it out to them…"

Duck took over, "I told them all recruits had to take a lick. Man, those guys shot out of that bathroom like greased lightning!"

24

Scraps of Laughter
for Ladies

There was a knock on the kitchen door. Boone opened it, and there stood Derwood. Again, he was shrouded in Duck's camo sleeping bag. His glasses were streaked as they balanced on the edge of his nose, and for all to see was the dried smear of brownie batter crossing the whole of his forehead.

On the last night of camp, after lights were out, Duck charged into the kitchen. "Where is Bro. Greg?" He was out of breath, and his eyes were wild. "I need him now!"

I dropped the dish towel I held, "Duck, what is wrong?" My mind raced. The only one we had ever had to take to the hospital was a Lubbock preacher and my own husband, but never a child.

"It's Derwood." Duck grabbed the hat off his head.

"What happened to Derwood?" I asked.

"Derwood wants to ask Jesus to come into his heart." Duck panicked, "Mrs. Sandy, I don't want to mess that up. I have to find Pastor Greg!"

Greg had stepped through the back door just in time to hear Duck's problem. A smile glowed over his face, "Let's not keep Derwood waiting, Duck. Where did you leave the boy?"

Duck blinked, "Huh, I'll go find him."

"We'll go find him," Pastor Greg corrected, and together they walked into the dark.

Later, when asked how Duck liked his first year as cabin Master Sergeant? In his own words, he smiled, saluted, and said, "Jr. Camp? Wow, it is great!"

Scraps of Laughter
for Ladies

Glass Doors

The world is certainly diverse, and the difference between even the closest people to you and you is tremendous. Take Greg and me. When we were dating, we fell madly in love. I think we just fell madly. Neither of us had a clue as to what 'in love' really was.

When Greg and I got married, we lived in a little two-room apartment in the church. He was assistant pastor, and it was a very big church building with hidden cubby holes everywhere. To get to our bathroom, we had to step out of our two rooms and traipse through a dark hallway that had two different groups of stairs, one going up and one going down. Plus, there were two around-the-corner spots in that hallway. Guess what Greg delighted in…you know it! He would hide and scare me every chance he got. I am so thankful I was young, and my bladder worked well!

When we finally moved into our house, it seemed like we had so much room. There were several different floorplans of homes in our neighborhood. Greg picked our floor plan while I was in my last semester of college, so I had never seen any of the other plans. You know the saying, 'Curiosity killed the cat?' Well, I am sure it did have something to do with a good portion of those nine lives allotted to the creature. One sunny afternoon, we were driving through our neighborhood and saw an 'open house' sign…of a house NOT like ours. I really wanted to walk through that home to make sure we had gotten the best floor plan. Greg agreed. To this day, I cannot remember what the house looked like. I only remember that as we left, the agent thanked us for coming, and I turned to walk out the open door. Only it wasn't open. It was a very clean glass door, and I face-planted right into that door. It was like a whole body slam you see on wrestling shows.

I bounced away from the door, trying to steady myself before I went down for the count.

Greg was the first responder, "Why did you do that?"

"What?" I mumbled.

Greg didn't ask if I was ok. He just wanted to know why I had run into the glass door…

I blinked, trying to catch my thoughts.

He repeated his question. "Why did you do that?" as if I had planned to run into the glass door! And I think he was embarrassed.

Spreading over the years, God blessed us with four kids. I remember the excitement when Greg announced he had a meeting to preach in Washington State. It was during the summer, so the family got to go with him. Yahoo! The maps were spread over the living room floor, and plans were made.

1. We visited a calm mountain lake. The kids canoed to the middle and dove in. I don't like water, and I cannot swim. So I watched with whitened knuckles from the shore. A lady strode up beside me and said, "You will want to check your children very carefully because this lake is full of leeches."

I felt a chill from the top of my head to the tip of my toes. "Leeches? I whispered.

"Yep, huge, blood-sucking leeches. And for your information, where their canoe sets, the water is about 20 feet deep. I trust they swim well." She turned and walked away.

"Greg!" I yelled, "We got to get the kids out of the water."

After I explained, Greg calmly put his arms around me, assured me the kids would be fine, and laughed about the leeches.

The girls did not laugh. They screeched as we searched and pulled leeches from their tender skin. Clay did the manly thing and tried to laugh it off.

2. Close to Tonasket, Washington, resides an old ghost town called Molson. It had been a gold miner's haven in its time. The family went to explore. Buildings stood like headstones, marking the spot as an ancient cemetery. The wind moaned through faded wooden walls from the surrounding trees. Among the buildings stood a bank, a cabin, a post office, a mercantile, an assayer's office, and a telegraph office. There we met a newspaper reporter writing a story on the Ghost town for the Seattle News. He asked our permission to take family pictures of our sightseeing tour throughout Molson. They sent us the centerfold spread of the Molson ghost town featuring our family. What a great memory.

3. Tonasket, Washington, happened to be close to Canada, and we decided to take a day and cross the border. We found a mall and began to explore. Everyone wanted a Canadian treasure. As always, Greg would rather find a place to sit and people-watch. The girls and I tried out every store the mall had to offer.

Scraps of Laughter
for Ladies

Now, I sometimes get turned around and lost in new places. I did. I was in a store and found a treasure I wanted Greg to see. I looked out the door and spied him sitting on a bench. I sat my treasure on the shelf and went to get him. I was well-aimed and had my goal in sight…when I ran smack into a glass wall. Stunned, I backed up and looked again…I blinked. That was not the doorway into the store. It really was a glass wall. Then my eyes landed on Greg. He had rolled over on the bench laughing, and all the kids had joined him in his merriment, pointing at me. Clay shrugged his shoulders, and I heard him say to a passerby, "I don't know who she is."

Along with the great meeting, those are the highlights of our Washington trip.

As a family, one of our favorite movies is called Prize Fighter, which features Don Knotts and Tim Conway. It is a slap-stick comedy, and there is an old lady who has lost her marbles crawling under a glass-top table barking at those who sit eating above her. With one accord, all the kids chided me, "That's going to be you, Mom! We are all going to get glass-topped tables, so you will have a comfortable place to eat when you and Dad come to visit!"

I rolled my eyes and moaned. Now, even our children had joined their father in laughing at me.

The next year, we were blessed to go to Ignacio, Colorado, and spend a few days in a Spanish-style retreat center. Inside there were bedrooms for each of the kids and best of all a swimming pool! The kids swam more than once a day. We could watch them through the glass walls of the swimming room. All

Scraps of Laughter
for Ladies

happened to be keeping vigil when our youngest, Kelloway, yelled, "I'll beat you to the pool!"
She tore out, running and smacked into the glass door. Kelloway bounced off and landed on her buns. Everyone laughed and teased, "Just like mom!"

Kelloway groaned, rubbing her forehead, "Who closed the door?"

The next day, Boone, Clay, and Tandolynn had a plan. Clay was to be in the pool, Boone by the door, and Tandolynn was to give the racing challenge, "Beat you to the pool, Kelloway!"

Of course, Tandolynn planned to let Kelloway win and while Kelloway was looking over her shoulder at Tandolynn, Boone shut the glass door to the swimming pool. Again, Kelloway ran head-on into that door. Her brothers and sisters will never let her forget it as they taunt her about being just like Mom, and maybe together, she and Mom could live under the glass dining table and bark at all who dare to sit there.

Greg and I have been married for forty-plus years now. When we hit the big 4-0, I asked Greg, "So…forty years…You know the Children of Israel were in the wilderness for forty years. Do you think things are going to get better?"

Greg laughed, "You mean like Jubilee?"

I raised my eyebrows and nodded.

And I must tell you…Jubilee has stepped in!

We were in Lake Havasu with the Rohns cooking steaks on the grill. They asked how I liked my steak, and I told them medium rare.

Bro. Rohn flipped the steak, "Uhoh. It might be too late for medium rare." Quickly, he forked the steak onto a plate, and Greg carried it into the house so I could check it.

31

Scraps of Laughter
for Ladies

Bro. Rohn called again, "Wait a minute, Greg. That one I just gave you will be yours. This steak is more… 'raw' the way your wife likes her steaks."

Greg had set the plate down, but he grabbed it right off the table, "Then this steak of mine needs some more fire." He headed back to the patio.

Now, the Rohns have a glass patio door. Greg had come through it and left it open. He either slams doors or leaves them wide open, but Bro. Rohn doesn't. I had watched Bro. Rohn through the kitchen window. He had gotten up from the grill and pushed the door closed, but Greg hadn't seen him shut that door.

A loud crash smashed the quiet, followed by a groan from my husband.

Greg had smacked right into that glass door.

I peeked around the corner. There stood my husband with a shocked look glazing his eyes and the plate and steak smothered on his belly.

Marge ran around the corner, "Are you alright?"

"Yeah," Greg paused, "I thought I left the door open. I guess I didn't.

I felt a giggle bubble up inside of me like springs of living water. By the time that water bubbled out it was a rolling waterfall of laughter. Oh, the Lord giveth sweet revenge! No longer do I regret all the glass things I have run into because…

Kindly, I smiled and asked, "Greg, why did you do that?"

Jubilee has begun!!!

Scraps of Laughter for Ladies

Especially for Beth Gosnell

Dear Diary,

I am writing to you, Dear Diary, so that I can wad this up, rip it in pieces, or send it through the shredder…and I would like to do the same with this day. It all started about 3:00 this morning when my husband yanked the covers off the bed and yelled, "Beth, wake up!"

I pulled my eyes open. He was standing on the bed, almost on his tip-toes, as far away from my side as possible.

"What are you doing?" I blinked.

He reached over and pulled the string for the light hanging from the fan above the bed. "Beth, in all our thirty-some years, you have never done this, not even when you were pregnant."

I was still groggy, "Do what, Dave?"

"You don't know? That is pathetic, Beth," he said, dropping to the floor and walking around to stand over me.

I reached toward the nightstand and grabbed the clock. "Three o'clock in the morning? Dave? I want to go back to sleep."

Dave was horrified, "In that?"

I squinted at my husband, "In what? The bed?"

"Ah, Beth," he reached over and touched my forehead. "You must be really sick. You wet the bed, like two gallons worth of wet. I am even wet on the side that was against you."

I gasped, "No way!" But a cold, damp feeling swept over me. I touched my red silk PJs stretched

33

across my buns. They were so wet that I think I could have wrung them out. I jumped out of bed and looked. The whole shape of where I had laid was shaded in wet. "I wet the bed? No way! I couldn't have wet the bed," I mumbled.

Dave headed for the bathroom, "Whatever you say, Beth. I'm jumping in the shower."

Those red silk PJs stuck to me like another skin. I peeled them off and sank to the floor to wait for Dave to get out of the shower. Sadly, I shook my head. "Fifty-some, and I wet the bed." Like a bolt of lightning, my head popped up, and I gasped. It had just dawned on me. I had not wet the bed. This was what women my age talked about: the plague of 'The Change of Life' commonly known as menopause! I yelled after Dave, "I did not wet the bed! It was only the Night Sweats!"

From behind the shower curtain, I heard him shout, "Gross! I'm sleeping on the couch."

And that, Dear Diary, was how my day started…and it did not get any better.

I work for a dentist, and I will not even tell you his name, Dear Diary. I will simply refer to him as Dr. Smith. I don't want a single solitary soul to find out his true identity, even though I intend to destroy you, Dear Diary! As my day progressed, we were in the middle of a root canal when someone turned up the thermostat. I know someone turned it up because Dr. Smith keeps it so cold in those rooms that all the rest of the workers wear long sleeves and layers. My face must have been next to purple, and a clammy mist crept over my whole body. I looked at Dr. Smith, waiting for him to ask who was responsible for this 105-degree sauna. Then he would say this was not the

Scraps of Laughter
for Ladies

time to be funny and to go turn the heat off. It didn't happen. Instead, he asked for more Novocain. I grabbed a needle and turned to hand it to him but dropped it to the floor. Dr. Smith laughed and called me klutzy. I glared. I was hot, crabby, and I had no sense of humor left, not even a pinch.

I knew, though, that there was no way I could leave a naked needle on the floor. Wildly, I tried pulling the glove off my damp hand. The sweat made it stick like glue. I pulled harder. Nothing. Finally, I yanked. To my horror, the glove freed from my hand, shot through the air, and swept across Dr. Smith's face. It clung for a moment on his nose and then slid to drop in the patient's yawning mouth. I gasped and snatched it out.

Quietly, Dr. Smith ordered, "Beth, go get Shelby to take your place. You take a break."

I didn't even argue. The fire burned inside me and sweat poured out of me. This had to be a HOT FLASH! I was mad and embarrassed. I stomped out of that room, hollered at Shelby, and tromped down the hall. As I passed an empty room, I had a great idea. I slipped inside, looked up and down the hall to make sure no one was coming, and closed the door. I ripped my smock off, dropped it in a pile on the floor, and snatched the hose that blows air to dry the spit out of patient's mouths. I shoved that hose down my blouse and turned it on full blast. It was like heaven. I closed my eyes and smiled, loving every moment of it. I was thanking the Lord for letting me work in a place equipped with machines that had the dual duty for menopause ladies when the door swung wide. My eyes popped open, and there stood Dr. Smith. His mouth

35

hung gaping. Slowly, he closed it and cleared his throat.

I looked. My blouse was billowing over my boobs. Like lightning, I ripped that hose out. The air end caught in my mouth, and I felt my upper lip flapping against my nose. I yanked the hose loose, lost my grip on it, and it flew snaking across the floor.

Quietly, Dr. Smith asked, "Beth? Are you okay?"

I pulled in a deep breath, licked my lips and stuttered, "I was…uh…I…uh…I was testing the equipment."

Dr. Smith chuckled, "And does it work well?"

I nodded, "Good pressure. Very good pressure."

Dr. Smith dropped his eyes to the floor and smirked at my waded-up smock.

Before he could comment, I muttered, "I guess I will just clean up." I turned off the hose, picked up the smock, and started for the door…

But Dr. Smith did not move. He cleared his throat again, "Beth, your husband called. He said he was worried about you. Something about you having an accident last night?"

My eyes were ready to pop out of my head, and I thought I might very well kill my husband! "He told you that?!" I shouted.

Dr. Smith held his hand in a surrender sign. Calmly, he spoke, "Beth, simmer down. Dave was worried about you."

"Worried? He had better be worried!" I threatened.

Dr. Smith took a step toward me and asked, "Was it a very bad accident? Are you hurt, and is your car alright?"

Scraps of Laughter
for Ladies

"Car?" I choked with relief. "Car?" I giggled. "Yes, the car is just dented a bit," I lied.

He continued, "Beth, why don't you take the rest of the day off and…here." He pressed a card in my hand. "Your husband asked me to give you this information."

In a trance I nodded. I held my head high as I walked past Dr. Smith and down the hall. I grabbed my purse from my locker and shoved out the front door. I clicked down the sidewalk, unlocked my car, slid in, shoved the key in the ignition, and turned it. For just a moment I sat behind the stirring wheel. I unfolded my hand and looked at the card Dr. Smith had slipped to me.

Free psychiatric evaluations
806-674-0879
Walk-ins welcome!

I gasped and looked up. There stood Dr. Smith at the glass door, watching me. He waved.

I yanked my car into gear and smashed the gas pedal. The car bucked and charged up over the curb. "No!" I yelled.

Dr. Smith started out the door, but I whipped that car into reverse before he could reach me and tore out of the parking lot. The last I saw of Dr. Smith, he was jumping over a dog I had almost hit and diving through the office door.

As I sped up the street, I rolled down the window, wadded up that card, and tossed it. I mouthed the word, "Menopause!" Just how long does this monster last? What will it cause me to do next? Will I survive? Will Dave survive? Will Dr. Smith survive? Maybe I did need that card! I stomped on the brakes. I needed that card! My life depended on it! A bunch of lives depended on it!

Scraps of Laughter
for Ladies

No Qualifications Necassary

Well, here I am again, Dear Diary,
This is the ad that I submitted to the paper this week:

Wanted badly: Person from 7:00 a.m. to 6:00 p.m.
NO QUALIFICATIONS NECESSARY.
On the job training.
Will interview in person at 1801 Magnolia.
Call for appointment, 592-0631.

Interview number 1

She came up the walk smartly dressed in a tailored, navy blue suit. She seemed hesitant as she rang the doorbell. When I swung the door open, her eyes widened.

"Excuse me," she said, "I surely must have the wrong address. I was coming for a job interview at 1801 Magnolia." She checked the paper again and looked at our house number.

I smiled. "No, Mam, you've got it right! This is 1801 Magnolia. Come on in."

Slowly, she crossed the threshold and stood.

"You can have the seat right here," I motioned to the couch and sat down myself. "Now, about this job," I began, but I could hear Snotz, our dog, barking up a storm in the backyard. I excused myself and went to the kitchen window to see what the problem was. The problem was Mickey and Boone. They were delighting themselves by spraying Snotz with the water hose. I yelled out the window, "Alright! You, two! If you don't leave Snotz alone, I will unchain him and let him have you for lunch! Do you hear me?"

Scraps of Laughter
for Ladies

Quickly, the boys turned the water off, and I returned to the living room to continue my interview with my first applicant. "Those boys!" I shook my head. "They seem to have a fixation with water hoses. The other day, they hooked my vacuum cleaner hose to the bathroom sink and sprayed all the walls and ceiling!"

Wide-eyed, my applicant nodded. She had picked up a magazine. Her head was tilted to one side, and her brows were scrunched together.

I looked over to see what she was looking at.

"Oh, that," I laughed. "Clay. He's going through the terrible twos. Still. We call him Marker Man. It seems he has this inborn radar for finding markers…mostly permanent black ones." I shook my head and asked, "Do you know anything that will remove permanent marker from permanent press?"

She shrugged her shoulders and asked, "About that job?"

But just then, little Kelloway woke up and started howling.

"Oh, excuse me," I said, "the dryer must have stopped."

She squinted her eyes at me, "What?"

"Well, you see," I started, but Kelloway continued to howl. "Just a minute, and I'll explain."

I ran to the dryer and turned it on. I sighed relief and went back to my Applicant.

"You see," I began as I returned to the room, "Kelloway is the baby. She is only two months old, and she has the three-month colic. I'm not really sure what the three-month colic is, but she cries all the time unless you bounce her. Finally, I discovered that if I put her on the dryer and turn it on…voila!" I snapped my fingers in the air. She sleeps. That discovery has been a godsend!"

My applicant's mouth dropped open, "You leave your two-month-old baby on the dryer?"

"Oh, it's okay," I explained, "I roll up a towel and lay it along the edge so she can't roll off."

"Oh," she grimaced and nodded, "about this job?"

It was then that Boone burst through the door yelling, "There's a Brontosaurus in the back yard!" He grabbed my hand, "Come on, Mom, you gotta hurry!"

"Not right now, Boone. Mama has company," I smiled.

"You gotta, Mom!" he persisted.

"NOT. RIGHT. NOW." I spoke quietly through clenched teeth and a plastered-on smile.

"Okay," he took out running. Then I heard him yell, "You all gotta come in 'cause the Brontosaurus gets the backyard!"

"No! No!" I yelled, jumping up. There was no way I wanted all those kids in the same room as my interview. "Excuse me," I smiled, "I'll be right back."

The Brontosaurus turned out to be a praying mantis scurrying through the grass, which we had to catch. It really was a big one.

As I came through the door I yelled to my applicant, "I'll be there as soon as I hammer holes in this lid!" Finally, I found the hammer on the bottom shelf of the refrigerator. Boone knew where it was. He had used it to peel carrots with the nail-pulling end because I wouldn't let him use a knife.

When the Brontosaurus was taken care of, I returned to my applicant. So did Boone. He crawled on her lap and shoved the jar in her face, giggling while she turned white and clasped her throat.

"What is it?" she gasped.

"It's harmless," I smiled, "only a praying mantis."

She swallowed.

"Want ta watch him eat a worm?" Boone asked.

She shook her head.

"Boone," I firmly stated, "Get down right now!"

As he slid off her skirt, he left a pile of wet grass and sand on her lap.

Everyone looked at the pile.

Boone had the solution. He ran to the closet. "I'll get the sweeper!" he yelled, yanking the door open and letting coats, football, baseball, and skateboard cascade out.

"NO! No vacuum sweeper!" she yelled right back while jumping up. I could see that she had visions of her tailored skirt being swept right off her body.

About that time, Tandolynn came prancing in, wearing nothing but her T-shirt.

My applicant gasped.

"Oh, Tandolynn," I moaned, "where are your skivvies?"

She smiled widely, "In sand pile."

"Honey, did you tinkle them again?" I asked.

She nodded her head.

"Where are you supposed to go to tinkle?"

"In 'mode."

"That's right." I continued, "You tinkle in the commode, not in your skivvies."

"That's when Boone added his two cents. "She didn't tinkle in her skivvies. She tinkled in Snotz's water dish, and he drank it! Yuk! That's why we sprayed him with the hose. We didn't want him to lick

Scraps of Laughter
for Ladies

us. GROSS!"

My Applicant sat down with a horrified look on her face.

"Excuse me," I smiled and scooped up little Tandolynn, "I'll be right back."

When I came back, Boone was settled cozily beside my applicant, saying, "...and Papa shoots mice right in the house with a real gun! And they splatter blood and guts all over the wall!"

"You're Dad?" my applicant's eyes were huge.

"No," I intervened, "Not his dad. His grandpa, and he lives 350 miles from here!"

I turned my eyes on Boone, "Now, Son, take little Tandolynn out into the back yard and keep her there!"

As they left a hush fell over the room.

My Applicant cleared her throat, "About that job?"

"Oh, yes," I said, "I'm thinking of going back to work, and I'm looking for a babysitter."

"A BABYSITTER?!" my Applicant shrieked.

"Yes," I calmly continued. "It would be just from 7:00 in the morning until 6:00 in the evening. The only meal you would have to fix would be lunch."

"Listen," my Applicant interrupted, "I don't have any experience concerning the area of children."

"That's no problem," I explained. "That's why my ad said that no qualifications were necessary. Really, it is on the job training, and you'll learn in no time at all. Why, Boone likes you already!"

Kelloway started screaming.

"Oh!" I moaned, "the dryer stopped! I'll be right back." I dashed to the laundry room and switched on the dryer. I smiled. It worked like a charm. Little

Scraps of Laughter
for Ladies

Kelloway tucked those fingers in her mouth and closed her eyes. I hurried back to the living room.

My applicant was gone! I ran to the door in time to see her jump the steps and fly down the walk.

"Oh, no," I breathed, someone had let Snotz out, and Snotz could never resist a running figure.

"Wait!" I yelled wanting to slow her down, but when she looked over her shoulder, she saw Snotz. She only sped faster. As she rounded the car, she paused to whop Snotz over the head with her purse. Snotz yelped, and she shrieked before she dove into the car almost headfirst. She revved it up, and wildly took out down the street never looking back.

I leaned against the door. Maybe if I could conduct my interviews somewhere else? But who could I get to babysit my kids?

Scraps of Laughter
for Ladies

The Flowbee

I was in a dilemma. Badly, I needed a pedicure, and just as badly, I needed my hair trimmed. Have you ever noticed that your own body doesn't do the things that you would like it to do, and it constantly does the things you don't want it to do? Right now, I wish it wouldn't grow my toenails so fast and keep chipping hunks of polish from the surfaces. At the same time, my hair had wildly escaped and was running tangent. Toenails and hair: I have been told they even grow for a while after the body has been put to rest six feet under. That must be scary, and it sure proves we are not in control.

Anyway, I checked my cash flow and found I only had the money for one grooming job. I studied my hair in the mirror. No longer would it do what I tried to get it to do. Instead, it hung limply about my face and seemed to drag the wrinkles into deeper and longer crevices. Yes, I had to get my hair done.

Then I checked my toes. They had those perfect growth marks causing white crevice moons between the toe and the polish. Many hunks and chips were calling, "Look at me!" When I was at home, it was no problem. Either Tandolynn or Kelloway would brush a bit of color on them, and both girls were good at that job. But I wasn't home. I was a long way from home. When I was young, I would paint my own toenails. Now I am not as agile, and I have this tummy bulge that gets in the way. Plus, my eyes are bad enough that by the time I get my foot close enough to see, my toenails are on the bottom side of my foot, and I would have to do the process upside-down. Once, and only

45

Scraps of Laughter
for Ladies

once, when I was penniless and desperate, I had my husband polish them for me. He brushed the polish on from side to side because that made more sense to him, and he didn't think anyone should be close enough to my feet to see that some of the ends of my toes were very colorful, too. I thanked him, but I never asked him to do it again. I thought my chances would be better if I painted them upside-down by braille.

Still, I stewed for several days. We were at my in-law's house when the solution peeked around the corner.

While sitting at the breakfast table, my mother-in-law said she was going to trim her hair today. I swallowed and asked, "You trim your own hair?"

"All the time. It's as easy as this," she snapped her fingers.

"Mmm," I thought. Her hair always looked nice. Maybe this is the answer to my dilemma.

Greg's mom continued to babble, "I saw it advertised on T.V. several years ago and ordered one. I've been using it ever since. It's called a Flowbee."

"A Flowbee? Does it work?" I asked.

My husband stopped his fork halfway to his mouth and gave me some kind of warning look.

His mom continued, "Sure. Like I said, I use it all the time. I used it on Greg's dad yesterday."

That should have been a red flag. Greg's dad is bald on the top, but he does have the ring-around-the-rim thing going, and I guess it needs to be cut just like any other hair."

Greg's dad was still chewing as I let my eyes wander across the table toward him. He never said a word.

Scraps of Laughter for Ladies

"And it doesn't take very long at all," my mother-in-law smiled. "Would you like me to trim your hair? I don't have anything going, and we could get it done quick as a wink."

This had to be God's answer to prayer. "Sure. I'll grab my clothes from the dryer and take them to the camper. I'll put on some grubbies and be back in a flash."

Greg cleared his throat, "I'll come carry those clothes for you, Hon."

As soon as we were out of ear shot he began, "Hon, I don't think that hair cut is such a good idea."

"Why? I need my hair cut. It won't do what I want it to do, and I am sick and tired of it," I told him.

"Then I'll take you somewhere, and you can get it cut," he told me.

"We can't. We do not have enough money to get my toenails done and a haircut, too," I whined.

"We'll find a way," he assured me.

"That could take forever, and I need it done now."

He sat the basket of clothes down and took me by the shoulders, "Let me explain something to you, Hon. My mom is always getting what she calls 'great deals' from T.V., radio, internet, friends, and you-name-it," he sighed. "And sometimes, they are not such great deals. She has been on a vitamin kick, a shake supplement deal, a make-up binge, a one-size-fits-all clothing market, and so many more. I can't even name them all. I don't know if you want to trust this…this…hair thing."

I paused for only a moment, "Flowbee. Your mom called it a Flowbee. And face it, your mom's hair always looks nice."

47

"I guess it does," he nodded.

"And I don't want to disappoint her now. You saw how excited she got. You know, this might help our relationship," I reasoned. My mind flew, and my heart started to pound a bit faster. Oh, yes, we had had a pretty rocky start. When we announced our engagement, she asked the whole church to pray that God would intervene so we wouldn't marry. Surely, that was a thing of the past. Hopefully, it was a thing of the past. Please, Lord, let it be a thing of the past. I swallowed. My mother-in-law was a beautiful lady. Her hair always looked nice…and I was pretty sure my father-in-law had always been bald.

I rubbed my temples.

Greg raised his hands in the air and stepped back, "Okay. You do what you want to do, but don't say I didn't warn you." He stepped out of the camper and slammed the door.

Suddenly, the quiet felt very loud. Was I doing the right thing? I went to change into my grubby clothes. I looked into the mirror. Yes. This was the right thing. My hair needed attention badly, and of course God was the one who had supplied this Flowbee answer. "Thank you, Lord," I whispered.

As I came into the house, my mother-in-law called, "In here, Sandy."

I stepped around the corner into the living room. She had a chair set in the middle. Greg sat on the couch, nursing a grin that spread from ear to ear. His mom stood with this apparatus in her hand. A long winding tube flowed down and was attached to the Hoover Vacuum sweeper.

I stopped and swallowed a gasp.

Scraps of Laughter
for Ladies

With a smile, Greg's mom said, "The vacuum sucks up all the hair, so there is no mess. You won't even need to shower when we are done. That was the selling point when I bought this wonderful Flowbee."

Greg winked, "Mom will have you beautiful in no time at all, Hon."

The death march. I could hear the death march playing as I tip-toed to the chair.

"How much hair do you want off?" she asked.

In a shaky voice, I spoke, "Oh, just a tiny bit."

The roar of the Hoover drowned any conversation, and I was glad. Vibrations spilled over my head as my mother-in-law drove that machine from side to side over my scalp as if she were combining wheat. When she was done, she flipped off the switch, and the silence was deafening.

I stared at my toes. They would probably have to wait to be professionally done because I was sure this Flowbee cut would need to be fixed professionally. Somehow, I would find a way.

Greg had quietly slipped to my side. I thought he was being sweet until he slammed a hand mirror in front of me. He was trying not to laugh.

That vacuum had sucked all my hair up to cut it off, and static electricity took over. There I was, hair wildly climbing to heights through wind currents unknown to man. It was like I had seen a ghost in an old horror flick.

Greg's mom was so sweet, "I could order you one of these miracle machines if they are still making them?"

Greg offered, "You could get it for her birthday, Mom."

"Oh, I will. What a good idea," she was elated.

Scraps of Laughter
for Ladies

I had to think of something quick, "Oh, oh, I am sorry, but it won't fit in the camper."

"It doesn't take up much room," she told me.

"But the Hoover vacuum would take up too much room, don't you think, Greg?" I sent him one of those 'you-had-better-agree-with-me' looks, and he picked up on it like a duck on a June bug.

"Awe, she's right, Mom. It won't fit in the camper."

My mother-in-law sighed, but she didn't give up. "Maybe they have a mini size. I'll check online."

Begging, I looked toward heaven. God knows my heart. Surely, there won't be such a thing online or anywhere else!

Greg eased his arms around me and whispered so only I could hear, "You look beautiful, Hon. How about a trip to town? A little ice cream fixes almost everything, and I hear they do hair at Walmart."

I love ice cream, and I sure prayed the Flowbee cut was included in the 'almost everything' ice cream would fix!

Scraps of Laughter
for Ladies

Dumpster Cat

We had just moved from a small, one-stoplight town in western Kansas, and that stoplight only worked during school hours. We had four children, the oldest nine and the youngest six weeks old. We were tired, and it was dark. The men of the church had come to help us unload. As the last boxes were set in front of the garage, a man asked, "Where would you like these, Mrs. Pastor?"

"You know, I don't know. Just leave them there until morning. I'll decide what to do with them then," I said, hoping I would be able to think again in the morning.

The man squinted at me, "Mrs. Pastor, do you want what is in those boxes?"

"Yes," I slowly answered.

"Then you had best not leave them out overnight."

That was my first clue we had moved into a shady neighborhood. The second came in the middle of the night.

We had set up the beds, and I had put my parents in the only bedroom with blinds. The rest of the room windows had wide gaping holes letting in the night terrors. Greg and I chose an upstairs room. It had a wall full of windows, but no blinds or curtains to keep the boogie men out. I turned off the lights to undress, crawled across the floor to the bed, dove in, and died to the world…until about three a.m.

Gunshots blasted, and I think the house shook. Greg threw the covers to the floor and jumped out of

Scraps of Laughter
for Ladies

bed, shouting, "Holy Toledo, what was that?" He ran to the window.

I gasped, "Get out of the window! There are no curtains! They can see you! That makes you a target!"

Quickly, he dropped to his knees, clutching the window sill, still searching the outer black. He whispered over his shoulder. "There is a guy standing under the street light. He has a gun, and I think he is shooting at that old Pontiac skidding down the street."

"Call 911!" I panicked.

"Honey, I can't. Our phones aren't hooked up yet."

Outside, a car revved and screeched to a stop.

"Besides," Greg whispered, "That kid just hopped in that souped-up, red Nova, and they tore out after the other car."

Greg padded back to bed and hugged my shaking body, "It's okay, Honey. God called us here, and He will take care of us."

I swallowed, "I want curtains. I need curtains!"

A few weeks later, our hunting dog, Buster, got out. We drove over the neighborhood...or 'hood' as we had shortened the word for our surroundings. It seemed to fit better. The kids were crying, and even Greg was teary-eyed. I missed Buster because I felt more comfortable with a big dog in the yard. Maybe we could replace him with a Doberman or a pit. But we didn't have to. A few days later, Buster wandered back, lugging his chain. But he brought a token of his travels. Tangled in his chain was someone's new bicycle. I smiled. Our dog had adapted to our 'hood' better than we had. He knew how to shoplift from people's yards without getting caught.

Scraps of Laughter
for Ladies

As time passed, we got more used to the 'hood.' The ministry was growing, and so were the kids. We knew certain things like you don't go out alone at night, don't talk to strangers, if someone tells you to hop in a car, don't do it, run when the souped-up, candy-apple red Nova makes its rounds, and the list went on. Each child had their chores and boundaries. They knew what they could get by with. Isn't that what boundaries mean?

I especially loved the evening when all the kids were in bed, and I relished a few moments of quiet. We had made it through another day in the 'hood'…safely.

I went into the kitchen for a glass of tea and groaned. Boone, our oldest son, was always pushing his boundaries. One of his chores was to take out the trash…and there it sat like a volcano that had spewed garbage over the edge of the trash can and onto the floor. I was fuming. "Greg, that kid will never learn," I said through clenched teeth. "He did not do his chore, and I think it is the second time this week!"

Greg was watching TV, so there was no answer.

I came around the corner to look at him. "Doesn't this bother you?"

"Huh," he mumbled.

"The trash, "I repeated. "Your son did not do his chores."

Greg's eyes were still glued to his cops' program. "Wake him up, Hon. Make him do it now. It'll be a good lesson for him."

I paused. "No. He has a test tomorrow, and he needs his sleep."

"Then let it set until tomorrow," Greg reasoned.

I tromped back into the kitchen and glared at the garbage. I was peeved, and it would serve Boone

Scraps of Laughter for Ladies

right to yank him out of bed. Yet, our streets at night were very unhealthy...ugly even! A volley of shots could be heard almost any night of the week.

Yet, I hated the trash. It seemed to be taking over my kitchen.

I decided to take out the trash myself. I grabbed debris from the floor and shoved it into the bag, stuffing it full. I yanked it from the trash can and hauled it through the kitchen, across the living room, and right in front of Greg.

Greg eyed me with a twinkle, "Thought you were gonna wait and have him take it out in the morning."

"It stinks. I cooked fish." I unlocked the front door and flung it open. I pulled the trash bag across the porch and down the steps before I hefted it over my shoulder. All the way up the street and over the parking lot, I thought of swats and or grounding our son until he graduated. The night air was cool, but it didn't cool me down. "For all I care, he can ride a bicycle until he leaves home!" I spewed through gritted teeth.

Even though it was a cool fall night, flies buzzed about the dumpster. I was glad someone had left a lid open because I hate to touch the filthy thing. I heaved that garbage bag over my shoulder, and with all my might, I swung it into the dumpster's yawning, black mouth cavity. I heard the bag give way and explode.

"Eegrech!" A horrible screeching belched forth like Night of the Living Dead! Two cats clawing wildly with hair flayed and teeth bared shot from the great dumpster's mouth.

Chills shot up my spine triggering a scream. And I ran, stumbling over the curb. I fell to my knees

Scraps of Laughter
for Ladies

and crawled madly across the street before I slowed down enough to get to my feet. In a frenzy, I tore toward the safety of my house.

The lone tree in our front yard was shaking, and I skidded to a halt. Behind me was the dumpster horror, and I didn't know what was ahead until... Billowing laughter erupted, and my husband, Greg, fell from the branches.

It scared the dickens out of me, and I yelled again.

Greg grabbed his belly, rolling in laughter, unable to utter a word.

I barged over to his shaking body and demanded, "What...just what...what do you think you are doing?" I stood over him, waiting for an answer, glaring, hands on my hips and tapping my toe in the grass.

Finally, he was able to put a sentence together. "I snuck out. I was going to scare you, but the cats beat me to it!" He tumbled into laughter again.

I dove in the middle of him, and we rolled in the grass. The tickling war had begun! Just when my husband had me pinned to the ground, that souped-up, candy-apple red Nova shrieked to a stop. The guy shoved his head out the window, gave a wolf howl, and yelled, "Way to go, Pastor!" Then that souped-up, candy-apple red Nova revved up and zoomed out of there, honking his horn.

And...

All the lights in the 'hood' flipped on!

Scraps of Laughter
for Ladies

I Was Only Gone For 24 Hours

The retreat had really been great. It was fun, relaxing, educational, and challenging. As I drove into the driveway, I paused. My little ones were playing in the sprinkler. I switched the engine off and looked at my watch. Yes, it was after 5:00 p.m. That is rather late for playing in the sprinkler, plus the fact that it was in the middle of March and there still aren't any leaves on any of the trees.

I stepped out of the car and was bombarded with hugs. It was good to be home, and I loved the hugs, but I badly needed to visit my bathroom. I ran into the house and flew to the bathroom. What a relief. I reached for the toilet paper and noticed that it was damp. Damp? I hesitated, smiled, and thought, 'Yes!' the sprinkler. The kids have been playing in the sprinkler, and they have gotten the toilet paper wet. Then I saw my flip flops by the bathtub. So, I stepped out of my heels and slid my feet into them. Yuk! They were soggy, too. I sighed and wished my kids wouldn't wear my flip flops in the sprinkler!

My husband was still sitting in his T.V. chair, "How was the meeting, Honey?" he asked.

"Really great." I waited a few seconds and asked, "How were the kids?"

"Really great. Didn't even notice 'em," he nodded.

"Honey," I bit my bottom lip. "Why are the kids playing in the sprinkler?"

"They wanted to, so I told them if they picked up all the popcorn on the floor, they could have sprinkler time," he said.

57

Scraps of Laughter
for Ladies

I could still see traces of popcorn over the room. "I thought you got movies for them to watch, honey." I tipped my head and looked at him.

"I did, but they said they'd rather play in the sprinkler," he explained.

"They did?" I was surprised. It was a big treat when we rented movies. Usually, you cannot pry them away from the T.V.

"Yeah. They watched part of one and decided they didn't like it," he shrugged his shoulders. "I liked it fine."

"What was it?" I asked.

"I don't remember the title, but it's right there on the T.V.," he motioned.

I was standing by the T.V. so I picked it up and read the title, "Son of a Gunman, the Saga of a Chicago Gangster who sets out to get revenge for the savage murder of his dog, Max." My mouth dropped open, "You got this movie for the kids to watch?" I demanded.

He shrugged his shoulders, "Honey, it's about a dog! Kids like dog movies."

I shook my head, "I'm surprised they didn't wake up scared to death last night."

He did not answer, plus he looked straight ahead at the TV.

"Oh, no! They did wake up scared, didn't they?" I guessed.

"Just the girls. They thought they heard machine guns," he chuckled. "I told them that it was probably Tandolynn's watch."

I raised my eyebrows in question. "Tandolynn's watch?"

My husband continued to explain. "Tandolynn

went to sleep with her watch on, and I guess she probably laid her ear on it and heard the ticking!"

I nodded, "Right. Did they go back to sleep?"

"Well," he began tapping his foot, "Yeah. With the light on and Tandolynn slept with her Bible under her pillow."

"Oh, Honey! I'm going to change my clothes." I headed to our room. When I stepped into the kitchen... I stopped. The remains of everything anyone had eaten or even thought about eating were all over my kitchen!

I smiled, "Honey?"

"Yeah?" he answered.

"Who fixed supper last night?" I questioned.

"Why?" He began to get defensive.

"Just curious." He really didn't have to tell me, I knew. There was a cheesy film all over the stove, a couple of boxes of macaroni and cheese, and the dirty pan. Our oldest son Boone knows how to cook two things: eggs and macaroni and cheese.

He decided to tell me.

"I had Boone make macaroni and cheese. I thought it would be a good experience for him, you know cooking and all. Besides, the kids like macaroni and cheese."

I sighed. Well, I definitely needed to change my clothes before I tackled the kitchen. I walked through the kitchen to the stairs and stopped. There in a pile was my navy dress, my Sunday navy dress with the white collar all in a pile. I picked it up and moaned. Smack in the middle of the white collar was the red lip imprint about the size of my youngest daughter, Kelloway.

"Honey," I called.

I heard him get up and head my way. He didn't

Scraps of Laughter
for Ladies

even flinch when he walked through the kitchen. He crossed to me, "You called?" He smiled.

I nodded and held the dress out to him. "Look at this. What happened?" I demanded.

"Don't look at me," he chuckled, "that isn't the size of my lips! You want to see?" He raised his eyebrows and leaned closer.

"No, I don't want to see. I want to know what happened to my dress!" I turned and headed upstairs. At the door of our room, I stopped and gasped. Half of my closet was scattered all over our room. "Just what happened here?" I asked in shock.

My husband came up behind me and put his arms around me. "I guess they didn't clean it up after they played dress-up."

"The girls? You let them play dress-up with my clothes?" I wailed.

"They said that you let them play dress-up all the time," he told me.

"Not with my clothes, I don't!" I shook my head and looked to heaven for help. One blade on the ceiling fan was gone, and the fan was going ker whap, ker whap, ker whap. "What happened to the fan?" I spread my hands and asked.

"Well," he hugged me tight, "It was really kind of funny."

I was about ready for something 'kind of funny!'

"Clay put on that little black thing of yours with the see through robe. You know that thing I really like you in?"

I nodded, "My teddy! They aren't even supposed to know I have it."

"Yeah. That's it. He put a pair of his red skivvies

on top of it, and then he tied the robe thing around his neck for the cape. Seems it's so featherweight that it flies behind him airy-breezy, like a Superman cape. He really liked that. Anyway, he was Batman or Superman or Zoro or someone and while he was jumping on the bed, he got it caught on the fan. But it's okay," he assured me. "I got him untangled."

"And my teddy?" I shook my head in despair.

"It's okay, Honey. I know you can fix it. You are magic with a needle and thread," my husband tried to soothe me, "And…he doesn't look anything like you do in it!" My husband tried to cuddle his arms around me.

I sank into the chair and gazed out the window. The bathroom rugs were draped over the back yard fence. I blinked. "Honey, what are the rugs doing on the fence?"

He sighed and knelt beside me. "The girls. They flushed something down the commode that didn't go down. It flooded the whole bathroom. But I got it fixed and cleaned up okay." He smiled and posed as a heavy weight, letting his arm muscles pop.

I dropped my head in my hands. Those were the things I loved about him! I sighed, and I dreaded even asking, but I had to know. "So, you washed the rugs and hung them out on the fence to dry, right?"

He laughed and looked at me like I was crazy, "No, silly, I didn't wash them, they were already wet! I just hung them out!"

I swallowed as the realization settled in. Slowly, I slipped my feet out of my soggy flip flops. That was not sprinkler water that soaked my flip flops or the damp toilet paper!

I shook my head and closed my eyes. I had only

been gone for 24 hours! That's all. Twenty-four hours!
It would take me a week to undo all that they had done
in 24 hours. I leaned back and closed my eyes. What I
needed, what I really needed, was another retreat!
But would I dare come back home?

Scraps of Laughter for Ladies

Goodwill #5

I sat on the floor in front of the fridge, searching in the lower depths for the "YUK" smell.

"Mom," the desperate voice of my sixteen-year-old daughter interrupted my search. "Mom, what am I going to do? I only have two pairs of jeans, and one of them is as old as 8th grade, and I only have seventeen dollars! What am I going to do?"

"Not a problem at all, Dear." I pulled out the hidden treasure I had been digging for and smiled. Last month's baked Alaska had grown a green tundra.

"Clay," I called. "Take this way out into the alley and dump it."

"Ahh, gross, Mom," he choked, "What is it?"

"What was it?" I corrected with a smile. "Actually, it is kind of neat. You remember that special Baked Alaska Aunt Cathy brought last month?"

Clay nodded.

"Well, it grew a tundra," I laughed.

"Really?" Kelloway poked her head over my shoulder.

"Well, duh," Clay shoved the dish under her nose.

"Perfect!" she exploded. " I need a good Social Studies project, and we are studying Alaska. Can I have it, Mom?"

"GROSS!" Clay gagged.

"Grow up!" Tandolynn groaned.

"I don't really think that is an Alaskan project," Boone chuckled. "Ten is so immature."

Scraps of Laughter
for Ladies

"What do you mean, it's not Alaskan? The name is Baked Alaska. That means it is Alaskan, right, Mom?" She stuck her tongue out at Boone. "See who's immature now."

"Okay," he laughed, "take it to school."

Kellow grabbed the dish, "I will, and I bet I get an 'A' on my Alaskan project."

"Enough of this! I am having a crisis!" Tandolynn exploded. "What am I going to do about jeans?"

I held my hands in the air. "Goodwill," I smiled.

Boone choked while chugging his glass of milk. He came up for air and laughed. "Tandolynn is going to Goodwill with Mom? This ought to be good!"

"Why?" Tandolynn softly asked.

Boone held his empty glass high and winked, "Because Mom tries things on."

"So? When you shop you try things on." Tandolynn watched her brother closely, "What's wrong with that?"

"They don't have dressing rooms at Goodwill," he chuckled.

"Mom?" Her eyes dropped to me in question.

"Over my clothes. I try them on over my clothes. I don't take anything off," I explained. "Besides I have to know it will fit."

She hesitated, "I don't know."

"Well, suit yourself, but jeans and overalls can be bought for two bucks and up," I spread my hands.

"Two dollars?" Her eyes sparked.

"Two bucks and up." I nodded.

She almost began to drool. "When can we go?"

"After school."

"Great." She twirled in a circle. "I can't wait!"

Scraps of Laughter
for Ladies

"I'll pray for you," Boone chugged the rest of his milk.

After school, she and I loaded with excitement, piled into the car. Goodwill #5 was only a few miles away, and in no time, we were in the store digging through the rack of jeans. There were a lot of 'maybes' and some 'If I have tos' until her eyes lit on the mannequin in the front window.

"Mom, what about that pair? That's the kind I like. Where are those kinds of jeans?"

"Well, they should be here with these jeans. I'll help you go through them again." We started rustling through them again. Nothing.

Depression crossed her eyes.

"Don't worry," I assured her. "Let's go check the window jeans."

Her eyes grew big. "You mean crawl up into the window?"

"It is only one step up, Tandolynn. People do it all the time."

She squinted at me, but we headed toward the window jeans. I unzipped the zipper to find the size.

"Mother! You are unzipping her right in front of everyone!" Tandolynn hissed in horror.

"Tandolynn. She is a mannequin. No one cares. No one will even notice!" I reasoned.

"Wrong." She motioned behind me where a group of kids had gathered, pointing and laughing.

Slowly I waved and sighed, "Children." I turned back to Tandolynn. "Listen. The size is perfect. I'll hold her up while you pull the jeans off."

"Mother. You have got to be kidding!" Her eyes grew wide.

Scraps of Laughter
for Ladies

"Tandolynn," I explained, "people do it all the time. Now I'll hold and you pull."

Tandolynn mumbled, "I cannot believe this!"

I took a deep breath and hefted under the mannequin's armpits. For one second, I felt like Zena, Warrior Woman, as I raised her high in the air. Then…she just flew apart. Her head shot through the air, hitting the show window. Both arms exploded in different directions; one zapped across Tandolynn's face, and the other landed in the lap of a woman in a wheelchair.

Silence settled over the store. All pairs of eyes rested on me as the manager headed my way.

"Yes?" she looked at me over her spectacles. "Do we have a problem?"

I smiled, feeling a red blush surge over my body. I was still holding the tummy of the mannequin. Even her legs had dropped and dragged the floor, as I explained. "These jeans are the right size for my daughter here."

The manager looked around for Tandolynn.

Tandolynn was gone!

The manager raised her eyebrows, "Daughter?"

I swallowed. "She doesn't like loud noises. She probably got scared and hid somewhere."

"I see." The manager nodded.

I licked my lips. "Is it okay to…uh…take the jeans off the mannequin?"

"Madame, you have taken almost everything else off the poor creature. Go on and take her jeans as well."

"Thanks," I sheepishly smiled. Quickly, I stripped off the jeans and laid the mannequin pieces in

Scraps of Laughter
for Ladies

a pile. I threw the jeans over my shoulder and began searching for my daughter.

"Tandolynn," I called.

"Shhh!" Tandolynn slipped from between the isles of dresses. "Mother, I cannot believe you did that!"

"Well, duh, Tandolynn. It is not like I decided to throw the thing everywhere. It just happened."

"Mom, I thought I would die! You embarrassed me!"

I shook my head. "Honey, worse things than that could happen. It's over. Just forget about it, and here's your jeans."

"Wow! Only four dollars!" she whistled.

"See, it was worth it, wasn't it?" I nudged her shoulder.

She giggled, "But I thought the lady in the wheelchair was going to have heart failure when that mannequin's arm landed in her lap."

"I thought I was going to have heart failure when it landed in her lap!" A wicked smile crossed my eyes. "I guess you could say I gave her a hand."

"Mother! That's a dad joke!" Tandolynn gasped at my joke, but she laughed.

"Now you've got your jeans." I patted the faded denim. As I turned, my eyes settled on the most beautiful dress I had ever seen. "Oh, Tandolynn," I breathed, "look at this." Gently, I caressed the silky lace dress. "This has got to have been someone's old wedding dress, maybe from the twenties. Isn't it beautiful?"

Tandolynn shrugged, "Yeah, Mom, it's really pretty."

Scraps of Laughter
for Ladies

"I cannot imagine ever letting it go to Goodwill. I'll bet that the bride of this dress died, and probably some daughter-in-law dumped it at Goodwill."

"Mother," Tandolynn shook her head, "you dream your dreams about antique wedding dresses, and I'll go look at the shoes."

I sighed and held the soft material to my face. I sized the dress with my eyes. "I bet it would fit," I whispered to myself. Quickly, I scanned the store for the manager. She wasn't in sight, so I unzipped the zipper and slipped the beautiful cloud of material over my head. "Yes!" With a little bit of wiggling, I tugged it over my overalls, sucked in my breath, and zipped. Boy, that waist was tight, but without my clothes beneath, it should fit perfectly. I knew this was mine if the price wasn't too high. "Please, Lord," I whispered, "let the price be in my range."

I began to unzip. The zipper went about six inches and stopped. I rearranged my arms and tried again. The zipper would not budge. I groaned. Tandolynn. I would find Tandolynn.

My eyes traveled over the store and rested on the shoes. Quickly, I moved in that direction. The tight skirt over my clothes made walking a little clumsy. I bumped into the Easter shelf, dumping plastic eggs as pastel hailstones over the cement floor. Like lightning, I ducked into a round clothes rack to hide as I watched the manager head in my direction. I held my breath. After she passed, I snuck out the other side and fell over Tandolynn.

"Oh, Mother," she groaned, "what are you doing?"

"I need your help, Honey. I am stuck in this beautiful dress."

Scraps of Laughter for Ladies

Tandolynn rolled her eyes at me. "Oh, she groaned. "Why did you put that scroungy thing on?"

"Because. And it is not scroungy. It is dreamy, but it is stuck now, and you've got to help me before the manager gets done with those Easter eggs." By now, I was pleading.

"Turn around," she ordered and began working with the zipper.

"Hurry!" I demanded.

"Suck in your gut."

"I am."

"Try harder!"

Finally, she shook her head. "It won't budge. Mom, we'll have to cut it off."

"No. Not this beautiful dress. I won't." I shook my head.

My daughter grinned. "Then you will have to take your real clothes off 'cause your dreamy dress is stuck to them."

I let out a deep breath. "I will not. I will buy the thing and wear it home."

"Mother, you can't."

"Tandolynn, I can't do anything else. I am stuck in the dress," I yelled.

"Yes? Is there a problem?" asked the manager from behind me while balancing an Easter egg in her palm.

I turned to meet her gaze.

"Oh, you again." Her eyebrows arched high.

"I...I...I want this dress. I think it is beautiful, and I think I'll take it home with me," I stumbled through the words.

She squinted over her glasses, "Would you like it in a sack?"

Scraps of Laughter
for Ladies

For a moment, I paused, then shook my head violently. "No. I like it. I'll wear it home."

In question, her eyebrows shot up higher.

Tandolynn came to the rescue. "She thinks some wonderful lady must have gotten married in this 'beautiful' dress, and my mom may never take it off again. She thinks it's good luck or something.

The manager chuckled while letting her eyes flow over me. Then she called over her shoulder, "Maggie, hey Maggie!"

An old lady with frayed, gray hair and black button eyes popped her head out of the back room. "Yeah, Maude, what do ya want?" she asked.

The manager smiled, "Maggie, I told you someone would buy this old dress of yours. Seems she thinks it is lucky."

The old lady gave a wide, toothless grin. Tobacco juice dribbled down her chin as she chuckled, "Why I'll be. It were a lucky old dress. Why, I married me first two husbands in that grand ole thing, and I would have used it for me last two if'n I hadn't spread so much. If'n you got marryin' to do, it's a good ole dress to do it in!" Maggie winked. "Why don't ya just give it to the lady, Maude?"

I could not wait to get out of Goodwill #5 and get home. In the car, Tandolynn refused to sit in the front with me, but she sure did not refuse to talk to me.

"So that's your dream dress, Mom." She laughed and made comments that she would never go to Goodwill #5, #6,#7, or #999 with me again.

I had had enough. I turned my eyes to the rearview mirror to talk to her. There was a lot about honor and obey she needed to know, and she needed to know it now.

Scraps of Laughter
for Ladies

"Mom!" Tandolynn shouted.

The light was red and I could not stop. I pushed on the gas pedal and sped through the intersection. I sighed with relief as we made it…until I saw the red light in my rearview mirror.

"This is not my day," I wailed as I pulled over and stopped. I threw my hands in the air and rolled down my window. I watched as the officer strolled to my car.

"Ma'am…" he began and stopped as his eyes dropped to my overalled legs hanging out of my new dress. I had pulled the tight skirt up so I could move my legs to drive.

The officer slid his 2-way radio off his belt and radioed his partner. "Frank, bring the camera. We've got a good one."

He turned back to me, "Ma'am, your driver's license, and, please, step out of the car."

I panicked. "But, Ossifler! I mean, Osclifer, I mean, Mr. Policeman! I can explain!"

He smiled. "I am sure you can. Please, step out of the car, Ma'am."

Slowly I opened the door.

Tandolynn slid down in the back seat.

Traffic pointed as they passed, and I thought I would die.

"Ma'am, have you had anything to drink?" the officer began.

I gasped. "No. My husband is a preacher. I do not drink. I don't even touch the stuff, Mr. Policeman." I had decided to avoid saying 'officer'.

He smiled at me and looked to his partner. "Frank, are you ready?"

Frank nodded.

Scraps of Laughter
for Ladies

"Ma'am," he looked at my license, "Mrs. Waggoner, please, walk down the line." He pointed.

"Which one?" I asked.

He burst into laughter.

I blinked. "There are two lines, a yellow one and a white one."

"Let's not try the yellow one in your condition, Mrs. Waggoner. Let's keep you as far away from traffic as possible."

"I am not drunk," I protested.

"Ma'am, just walk the line."

My anger was kindled. I stood tall, straightened my beautiful skirt over my overalls, waddled to the line, waddled down it, and turned back to face the officer.

"See, Osslefer! I am not drunk!"

Another car went by, honked, and waved.

Finally, I convinced them I was not a drinking woman. They seemed even to think the situation humorous enough that they sent me home with a warning.

As we drove in the driveway, I warned Tandolynn. "Don't you dare tell your dad or anyone else about this."

Tandolynn groaned. "Do you think I want to ruin my image? I just hope none of those cars driving by recognized you."

Months went by, and all was well until one evening, my husband yelled, "Honey, come quick!"

I stepped into the living room in time to see some lady in an old, beautiful dress bound tightly around overalls shout, "See, Osslefer! I am not drunk!"

The show COPS was on T.V.

72

Scraps of Laughter
for Ladies

Mini Pads

More than anything, my teenage daughters did not want to be like me. It wasn't that they didn't like me. They love me. It's just that I am their mother. I remember a comment someone made at church about Tandolynn looking like me while she was in her sophomore year of high school. I could tell by the look on her face that it did not sit well. She promptly took her friend, Norma Leigh, with her to a beauty shop and had her hair cut. She danced in when she got home, "So what do you think, Mom?" Tandolynn's bobbed hair bounced as she twirled.

I laughed, "Tandolynn, your hair is adorable. That's so funny because that is exactly how I wore my hair in high school, and I think it was my Sophomore year, too."

Tandolynn gasped, "No, you didn't!"

I nodded my head, "Yes, I did."

"Really?" her smile faded.

"Really, and I have the picture to prove it. I'll show you." I ran up the stairs to my bedroom and dug the photo out of an old album.

When I returned, Tandolynn was still standing dazed in the middle of the living room with her friend Norma Leigh.

I swished my sophomore photo in her face before I shared it about the room.

Clay latched onto the picture and rolled in the floor. He laughed and added, "Yep, and your hair is the same color as Mom's. You look just like mom!"

Tandolynn glared at her brother.

Scraps of Laughter
for Ladies

I took the photo and shoved it into her hand, "See?"

Norma Leigh giggled, "Tandolynn, your mom looks just like you!"

Tandolynn groaned, grabbed Norma Leigh's arm, and headed back to the beauty shop together. There was no way she was going to continue to feel warm and cozy with the 'mom' cut. She pranced in when she came home, saying, "I'll bet no one thinks we look alike now." Her hair was shorter and colored red.

As the high school years passed and work began, the girls didn't mind looking like their mom so much as the weird quirks they seemed to acquire, which had 'mom' written all over them. They weren't weird. They were things no one else's mom did, like tripping on the yellow line in the pavement.

Years passed, and Kelloway was now a newly working woman when she came into the house and dropped her coat. She sank onto the couch, slipped off her shoes, and threw her feet up, "Mom, I have an idea."

I stepped out of the kitchen, "Shoot."

"I have Monday off. Why don't you take the day from your second-grade class, and I'll drive you to Haven, Kansas? Do you think we can surprise Dad?"

It sounded like a wonderful idea to me. Greg had been in evangelism for about two years, and I was still teaching school. He had been gone for three whole weeks with two more to go…and…believe me, that was a long stretch of time. I was convinced. I called in and took Monday off!

We live in West Texas, and the drive would be through Oklahoma and Kansas. All the towns along the

Scraps of Laughter
for Ladies

road were dinky, dying towns, but Stratford, Texas still had a Dairy Queen. I love ice cream. I believe ice cream will be in Heaven, and we must have a taste of Heaven every time we drive through little Stratford, Texas. With joy and tummies cheering us on, Kelloway and I made the ice cream stop. I ordered my favorite blizzard, Turtle…or…pecan cluster…with a bit of the extra hot fudge. The boy at the counter was in high school. He grinned and assured me there would be plenty of turtle goodies in my special blizzard.

Finally, the young man sat our blizzards on the counter, smiled, and told me how much money it would be.

Now, when traveling, I have a special envelope for my travel money. This was my treat, so while I chatted with Kelloway, I fished in my purse for my money envelope. We were so involved in the conversation that when I pulled out my travel envelope, I slipped out a twenty and handed it to him without looking. Kelloway's eyes deepened with horror, and her face drained of color.

Still, without looking, I laid the bill in the young man's palm concerned about Kelloway, "Honey, are you okay?"

She paled even more and shook her head, "I'll wait in the car."

I watched her almost run from Dairy Queen before I turned to the young man still holding the twenty.

I gasped. IT WAS NOT A TWENTYT WAS A MINI PAD!

I had grabbed the wrong envelope!

His face was a mass of pinks and purples, yet his eyes reserved a twinkle.

Scraps of Laughter for Ladies

All the customers had quit talking and were staring at me.

"Oh! Oh! Oh! I am so sorry! Wrong envelope!" I stammered. I reached across the counter, whipped that mini pad out of his hand, and stashed it in the depths of my purse. "I am so sorry!" I swallowed and began digging again. "I know I have the right envelope in here, somewhere, with my money in it."

The young man cleared his throat and wiped his hands down the sides of his apron, "Ma'am, the manager just said to tell you the blizzards are on the house."

I looked up. Behind the order window, the manager grinned, tipped his little Dairy Queen beanie, and winked.

I stumbled through a thank you, grabbed the blizzards, and headed for the door.

In the car, Kelloway rolled her eyes. "Mother, why did you do that? You embarrassed me. And I am telling you right now, THAT WILL NEVER HAPPEN AGAIN! The next time we hit Dairy Queen, we go through the drive-through!"

I raised my eyebrows, "Kelloway, you can't think I did that on purpose. I just pulled out the wrong envelope."

Kelloway whipped her hand out and demanded, "Give that envelope to me now. There is no way I'll let this happen again."

"But what if I need a mini pad?"

"You can ask me for one, but not in public." She warned as she shook her head. "Mother!"

I narrowed my eyes and laid out the facts for her. "Someday, Young Lady, you may be just like me."

Scraps of Laughter
for Ladies

"Never." She revved up her car, and we tore out from the driveway of Dairy Queen in Stratford, Texas.

A few years have passed since that day. I took early retirement to travel with my husband. I couldn't stand life without him. I guess Miss Piggy and Kermit have a song that fits: 'You Can't Live with Them, and You Can't Live Without Them.' But for the record, Kelloway has no control over my mini pads, for which I am sure she is very grateful….as am I. And Mini pads have come a long way. They can be bought individually wrapped in pretty color-printed paper. This is great because I can slip one into my pocket should I want one while we travel. No one ever needs to know what it is if I should accidentally pull it from my pocket because it is wrapped so cutely.

A couple of months ago, I searched pockets before I tossed in a load of laundry. Sure enough, my skirt pocket had a few coins, a couple of dollars, a Chapstick, and a daintily wrapped mini pad. I smiled as they always bring to memory that special Dairy Queen, the 'blizzard on the house,' and my daughter, Kelloway. I turned it over in my hand and noticed something sticking out of the plastic paper seam. I pulled. Out came a small slip of paper from a Chinese fortune cookie. It read, "You will be unusually successful in an entertainment career." I laughed. We had eaten at some 'Hi Flung' restaurant, and I had stashed the fortune from my cookie into my pocket with my other goodies. But…What an idea: mini pads with fortunes in them! Maybe I could make a fortune! I texted both my daughters with the story, and we all had a good laugh. (Yes, Kelloway can laugh about it now.:-))

Scraps of Laughter for Ladies

I was feeling kind of home sick last week when Kelloway called just to let me know she had been jogging in the frozen drizzle of South Dakota. I told her she had better be careful because she might slip and fall. Kelloway laughed, "I already did, but not because it was slick. I tripped over the sidewalk crack."

I laughed, "That sounds like something I would do."

"I know. Thanks, Mom."

That same day, Tandolynn texted me. The message was a mass of capital letters that said, "THANK YOU, MOM!"

I texted back, "You are quite welcome I am sure, but thank you for what?"

She texted back, "I just tried to pay the cashier at the grocery store with a mini pad! Mom! The lady handed it back and told me I could check with their manager if I wanted, but as far as she knew, their store does not accept that kind of bill."

"Congratulations!" I texted. Both of my girls had experienced the worst of the worst, or so I thought.

A couple of months ago, I got a text from Tandolynn saying, "Call Me!!!!"

So, I did.

"Mother!" she almost yelled over the phone.

"Whoa, are you okay, Tandolynn?" I asked.

"No. Just how could I be okay? I inherited you!" her voice was shaking.

"Calm down, Honey, "What happened?" I spoke quietly.

"What happened?" her voice cracked. "I'll tell you what happened. I was in Walgreens checking out at Dominic's counter. We were catching up on high school, and I was trying to write a check. I needed a pen, so I dug in my purse for one. Finally, I found my pen in the debris of the lower depths and drug it out. Dominic had just asked me if there were any 'special' men in my life. I said, 'Well…' you know, like I was giving the matter thought, and let my eyes roll toward the ceiling. Then, with a feminine flourish, I stuck the end of my pen into my teeth to pull off the cap to write my check…Mother! I thought I was going to die! I was trying to write my check with a tampon!"

"I love it!" I told her with tears rolling from my eyes.

We laughed, but I laughed more! Oh, yes, my girls are going to be just like me! The good, the bad and the ugly!!! :-)

Scraps of Laughter
for Ladies

Oil of Olay

When I was a girl, I remember lazily resting my head in my hand while lounging against the bathroom cabinet. My Grandma Doshia was generously rubbing cream on her face. "Now, Sandy, she smiled and winked, "if you start while you are young and use this miracle cream called 'Oil of Olay' faithfully, you'll have a face like mine. It's as soft as a baby's bottom." She patted her cheek.

I didn't say a word, but I thought that would be the last thing I would use, considering the fact that my Grandma Doshia's face was a road map of wrinkles, and there was no way I wanted mine to be described as anything resembling a baby's bottom.

Years later, I shook my head as I remembered that moment in time. I stood before Walgreens's Oil of Olay display of 'guaranteed to make you look younger' products. I had decided I needed eye cream. My eyelids had been itching, so they must be that 'old' dry, which comes before 'droopy' dry. The bags beneath looked like they were packed…bulging even, and ready for a road trip. Without squinting, I could see little crow's feet trampling from the corners of my eyes clear to my hairline. As much as I hated to admit it, it was time for the Oil of Olay. I grabbed the eye cream and headed for the register.

That night, I turned my back on my husband and switched out the lights. Quietly I screwed the lid off the jar and dipped into the rich cream. I spread a lush portion of the miracle 'crème de la crème' around my eyes, closed the jar, and snuggled beneath the covers to sleep.

Scraps of Laughter
for Ladies

"You don't need that, you know. You are beautiful," My husband wrapped his arms about me.

I giggled, "How did you know?"

"I know everything," he whispered, "And I watched you in the mirror in Walgreens."

I jabbed him with my elbow. "You had better call for an eye doctor appointment tomorrow."

The next morning was Sunday. My husband always wakes the family, and they tumble into our room to pile onto our bed for devotions. It's a good thing we have a king-sized bed, but they love the time. We all do, and I get to stay snuggled under the covers longer. This Sunday morning, I could hardly drag my eyes open. We had our devotions, prayed, and the kids zoomed to the kitchen for Sunday cereal. Then, my husband took a moment to accuse me of snoozing through devotions before he left for church, suggesting I might visit the altar. I laughed.

Finally, I dragged myself out of bed and trudged to the bathroom for my shower. I pulled up to the sink and looked in the mirror to examine how my new wonder cream had worked. I gasped, "OH, NO!" I panicked. My eyelids were purple and swollen so much they drooped halfway over my eyes. No wonder I couldn't get my eyes opened. I doused them with cold water, but no luck. I jumped into the shower and gently patted my eyes dry. Still, no luck! The bags beneath my eyes now looked as if they had been packed for a whole summer vacation.

For church, I tried to cover them with eye shadow, but it looked like I had been in some brawl at a shady place on the boulevard. I sat in the back during church and tried to sneak out after the final amen. It seemed the pastor's wife could not sneak! I laughed at

Scraps of Laughter
for Ladies

the many comments I received and told the concerned parishioners my week at school had been rough, as test weeks always are.

To my despair, on Monday morning, my eyelids still bore the signs of the miracle cream brawl: Oil of Olay. Through the many comments from my co-workers at school, I calmly replied, "Rough week-end." No telling what they imagined had happened at church, and I knew how happy it would make my husband...if...he found out.

By now, I had figured I must be allergic to the Night of Olay, and one would have thought I would have thrown the stuff, the wonder serum, Crème de la crème, into the trash. Truly, I intended to. I rolled the little, expensive jar around in the palm of my hand, but I just couldn't part with it yet. I tucked it into the depths of my nightstand drawer.

A few months later, I discovered it was not really the eye cream I was allergic to. The culprit had been a stick of new mascara. So, I dug in my drawer, pulled out the miracle stuff again, and joyously applied it. Now, those tell-tale crow's feet could march into oblivion. The morning revealed that no such luck existed for me! My eyes were even more purple and swollen than the last time.

Again, it was Sunday, so I wore a hat to shade my face and looked at the carpet when I talked to people. However, while sitting in church, the light went on! I had a scientific idea. The miracle cream caused a bit, or in my case, a lot of swelling. That must be how it conquers the wrinkle problems. It just swells the wrinkles right out of your skin. And...I noticed that my upper lip was starting to show a bit of age. Science! I could do my own science experiment.

Scraps of Laughter
for Ladies

Instead of tossing the cream in the trash that night, I rubbed a healthy hunk of it on my upper lip. The next morning my lip looked great. Truly, I discovered the Oil of Olay to be a miracle cream! It worked for my upper lip instead of my eyes. I continued the experiment all that week.

Then my husband tried to dark walk on my side of the room and put something on my bed stand. He yipped as he knocked over my glass of cold water…mostly on him. I laughed. Later, I groaned. He had also lost my Magic Cream. I had to dig under my bed for my miracle treasure.

But all the while I dug, I had this tugging feeling that God, himself, might be trying to tell me not to use this stuff again. I wadded up that thought and tossed it away. After all, this was my face we were talking about, and everybody saw that. I had the right to make my appearance the best, so I had to find that bottle of Olay. I dropped to my hands and knees. I squeezed the front half of me under the bed, hoping no one would come view the back half from behind. I dug into the darkest, untouched recesses until I finally found my treasure. I clasped my fingers tightly around the little jar. It felt cold in my hand, but way back in the hindermost part of my mind, there was again that tiny nagging, an inkling that something was not right. I ignored it.

The next morning, groggily, I pulled my nighty over my head and stepped into the shower. When the water hit my face, I noticed my upper lip felt numb. I rubbed my lip. Nothing. I pinched my lip between my fingers and pulled, stretching it way out from my face. Still…nothing! I did not feel a thing. When I let go, my lip bobbled for a moment before it sagged back

Scraps of Laughter
for Ladies

into place. I grabbed my towel, jumped out of the shower, and swiped the terry cloth over my face and then the foggy mirror. I leaned close to the reflection. My top lip was swollen and drooping over my bottom lip. Splotches over my upper lip were flaking off! I raked my fingers through my hair. What was I to do?

Before I left for school, Greg walked me to my car. When he and bent down to kiss me, he stopped midway, "Whoa! Is that contagious?"

I shook my head which flopped my lip. Greg backed away from me, and before I could come up with an explanation, he leaned in and kissed me on top of my head. Then he backed further away and wished me well.

My second graders were very concerned. "Mrs. Waggoner," Natalie offered, "I'll watch the class while you go to the nurse's office."

I smiled, "I'll be fine, Natalie." As the morning passed, I found all the kids watching me closely. Little Harold drew quite a picture of me and for me. I looked like a duck!

Later, I sent Natalie to the office with a head count for the upcoming field trip. When she came back, she had the school nurse in tow. I took a deep breath and stepped over.

Mrs. Godfrey, the nurse, lowered her spectacles and pursed her lips together while examining my lip. "Mrs. Waggoner, it looks like a reaction to Botox injections."

I gasped and grabbed her arm to pull her outside the door. That was something second graders didn't need to hear. I swiped my hand in a circle around my face, "This…I assure you, this is not Botox!"

Scraps of Laughter
for Ladies

Karen, the teacher across the hall, stuck her head out and winked at me just before she closed the door to her room.

Mrs. Godfrey shrugged, "Whatever you say, Mrs. Waggoner, but I would swear on a stack of Bibles that lip has tasted Botox. Oh, pardon the expression, beings how you are a preacher's wife...of course that would mean you don't lie..." She turned and clipped down the hall.

I gasped, "No, I do not lie."

She chuckled, but she didn't turn around, and I knew it would be all over school before the day was over.

As I stepped back into the classroom, Natalie asked, "Mrs. Waggoner, what is Botox?"

All the kids stared at me as I explained, "It is a vitamin that helps build muscles."

Jacob's eyes were huge, "On your lips, Mrs. Waggoner? WOW! It really works."

Brandon burst into the conversation, "Your lip kind of flaps when you talk, but I'll bet Mr. Waggoner really likes that muscle!"

I swallowed, "Yes. Yes, he does."

After that long, horrible day, I drove to the middle school to pick up Tandolynn. As she scooted into the front seat, she froze, "Mom, what happened to you?"

I shrugged my shoulders.

"Mom. Did you go to school like that?"

I nodded.

She swallowed. "Mom, in health class we saw this film," she paused, "only for girls. It tells you what causes things like that. Do you want me to ask my teacher if I can barrow the film for you?"

Scraps of Laughter
for Ladies

"No!" I gasped.

When I got home, I marched to my nightstand, grabbed the jar, and threw it in the trash. By now, I knew God had been trying to get a hold of me, but I hadn't been answering the phone. This time, God had used the fire alarm, maybe a tornado siren. Yet, as I gazed at that expensive, little miracle jar in the trash surrounded by waste, a part of me still wanted it. Slowly, I reached down and fished it out to cradle it in my hand. Oh, I promised myself I would never use it again, except as a reminder of my Grandma Doshia and to remember that when God does truly talk to his people, you had better listen.

To this day, that crème de la crème, that miracle serum, that wonder cream, Oil of Olay, has a special place on my shelf and in my heart, but never again on my face!

Scraps of Laughter
for Ladies

That Black Shetland

"Oh! Yuk! Gross!"

My sister Cathy and I giggled. We were underneath the bleachers at the sale barn, and some gross guy had just spat a wad of tobacco, juice and all. It splattered right between the two of us. We both gagged and jumped aside. One step closer, and Cathy would have been wearing the slimy wad. Quickly, we scrambled up the bleachers to where Mama and Daddy sat.

Coming to the sale was always a highlight and something we only got to do in the summer because the sale was always held on Fridays. Today's sale was to be special, one we would remember for the rest of our lives.

We woke up early to Daddy's tap on our door, and he always call, "What do you want to do? Sleep your life away?" Sometimes, we did want to try to sleep our lives away, but not today. We had the sale barn to look forward to. We got to gather, sort pigs, and load the critters for the sale. We tumbled out of bed, and our adventure began.

Pigs were on the docket to sell first, and then the cattle sales began. It was in between the pigs and the cattle that the shiny black stallion pranced into the ring. My brother Larry, Cathy, and I loved him at first sight. My heart danced. That black horse was so shiny that his coat reflected iridescent shades of the rainbow as he danced about the ring. He was so little and cute. The fact that he was a Shetland only made him more appealing to us. He was just our size, maybe not Larry's size, but definitely Cathy's and mine.

89

Scraps of Laughter
for Ladies

We tumbled down the bleachers to where Mama and Daddy sat. We began begging for that piece of horse flesh. Daddy's smile lighted a glint in his eyes. I think Daddy knew something we did not.

Daddy bid and bought that black Shetland for a mere forty bucks. The owner took off his hat, wiped the sweat from his brow, and threw in the reins as a gift.

We asked no questions. We were so happy, and we couldn't wait to get him home, put those reins on him, and ride.

We rubbed and petted him through the side rails in the back of the pick-up. That black Shetland watched us out of the corner of his eye and kept chewing the handful of green weeds we had found, pulled, and offered to him.

We begged Daddy to let us ride in the back of the pick-up with our newfound prize, but Mama gave a firm 'no,' and Daddy's eyes twinkled as he agreed with Mama.

Larry, Cathy, and I agreed on the name Midnight because our Shetland was so black he glinted in the sunlight.

We couldn't wait to climb on Midnight's back. When we got our Shetland home and unloaded, Larry claimed the right to the first ride. After all, Larry was the oldest and most persuasive, and he always got to do everything first.

Larry grinned with victory and swung his leg over Midnight's back.

Cathy and I felt sorry for midnight. Larry was so tall, and Midnight was so short that my brother's legs almost dragged the ground. Poor Midnight! Cathy and I giggled. Larry and Midnight looked like a six-legged creature. We even thought of names like Midlar or Larnight.

Midnight just stood flicking his ears.

"Come on," Larry coaxed and nudged the horse's sides with his legs.

Midnight stood like a statue.

Larry furrowed his brows and kicked that Black Shetland.

Midnight laid his ears flat, rumbled from deep within, and lunged into a full-fledged stampede.

Larry howled a "Yee Haw!" and they were off!

Midnight headed straight for the clothesline.

Larry's eyes popped wide, and he yanked back on the reins.

That Black Shetland paid no attention.

Larry ducked, gluing himself to the horse's back as the hanging clothes parted way for him. A frilly blouse caught about Larry's neck and flowed after him as Midnight's mane flew behind him.

Then Midnight tore out toward Stausser's hedgerow. That Black Shetland ran under every low-hanging branch in that hedgerow trying to rake Larry off his back. Our brother was just as stubborn as that Black Shetland. He somehow wound the reins around his arm and his arms around Midnight's neck.

As they turned to barrel back to our house, Cathy and I tumbled up the porch steps. We wanted to be out of the way.

Midnight slid to a halt, dipped his head, and Larry slid over the horse's head, landing on his feet.

Larry smiled, gathered the reins, and led Midnight to the porch. Our brother had victory written all over his face as he asked, "Who's next?"

Scraps of Laughter
for Ladies

It was then that Midnight stealthily stretched his neck to Larry and bit a hunk out of his back. Larry's mouth flew open with a Texas yell of pain. That Black Shetland rolled his horse lips back, bearing his big, yellowed teeth, and laughed.

Cathy and I flattened our backs against the door as far away from that Shetland as possible. Neither of us wanted to ride that horse, and he wasn't so beautiful anymore. We didn't even want to get close enough to pet him.

As the summer wore on, Larry still rode that Black Shetland. I think he had a lot of Shetland qualities himself, and in some odd way, they liked each other. Sometimes, Midnight would stroll lovingly toward Larry and gently set his foot on top of Larry's foot. Then that black Shetland would shift all his weight to that foot and snort with horse laughter. About August, Midnight discovered a new trick. He would run like he was flying out of the starting gate. When he hit full blast that horse would dip his head and lurch to a stop. Larry did not stop with Midnight. He was launched, airborne, flying until his whopping big landing. Dust plummeted about him, like in the Western movies. Midnight would strut just out of reach, turn, peel his lips back, and laugh. I was surprised my brother did not kill that Black Shetland. Or, maybe he tried, but Midnight's head was just too hard, and…maybe that was their bond!

When school started that September, Larry had to leave early, and he was in football, so he came home late. He didn't have time to feed Midnight or to ride him, so their relationship ended. That relationship was passed on to me. I was to feed that Black Shetland every day before school.

Scraps of Laughter
for Ladies

Some crazy person placed the feed bunk in the middle of the corral. I don't know whose idea that was, or maybe my brother did it before he turned over the chore to me. I would have put it against the fence so I would never have to step in the pen with that Black Shetland.

As it was, I would sneak to the gate and locate Midnight. Then, I would mentally map out a route to the feed bunk away from that Shetland. Before I dared open the gate, I would calm my heart and pray because I still remembered the look on Larry's face when Midnight bit a hunk of his skin from off his body. Larry's feeding method had been easy for Larry. He hadn't been scared, but then his legs were as long as Midnight's. He didn't have to be scared. If Midnight snuck up behind him, Larry would simply knock him over the head with the feed bucket, and Midnight could eat his feed off the ground.

My method involved a lot of running. I was always too busy running to aim the feed bucket. After I had built up enough courage to open the gate, I would wildly dash to the feed bunk and dump the feed. If all went well, I would run back to the gate and slam it behind me. There were times I had no time to open the gate, so I would madly dive over the fence. If all did not go well, I would be treed in the middle of the feed bunk with Midnight trolling around the bunk. That Shetland's teeth would be bared as a mad dog. His tail would twitch, and his ears were laid low. He would snort, and he would stomp. I knew he wanted a hunk of my hide or one of my fingers.

While standing in the bunk, I would sweet-talk that Black Shetland telling him how nice he was and that I was not afraid of him.

Scraps of Laughter
for Ladies

He did not believe a word I said.

I spent many hours in that feed bunk lying to that Black Shetland, and I don't know how many times I was late to school.

I had cousins that came to visit. Beck lived on a farm with real horses. She bragged that she could ride anything with four legs, so I let her. She saddled that Shetland; Midnight's ears twitched. She climbed into the saddle; Midnight snorted. She took the end of the reins and whapped his backside; Midnight stomped. She whapped and kicked at the same time; Midnight lunged into a wild run! They flew across the grass and into a plowed field. Then Midnight dipped his head and lurched to a stop; Beck didn't. Midnight rolled back his lips and laughed; Beck didn't...but I did!

Finally, Daddy decided we weren't paying enough attention to poor Midnight, and I suppose I kept 'forgetting' to feed him. It was a good thing Beck was our cousin and did not sue us, so Daddy moved him to the farm. He put that Shetland in the same pen with the biggest, meanest sows you ever saw. I was relieved!

Then, one night at supper, Daddy made the announcement. Midnight had to go. That Black Shetland had chased down nearly every sow and had bitten off their tails.

I looked down at my fingers with wide eyes and thought of all the close calls I'd had. I was right! That Black Shetland had wanted my fingers!

Friday, we loaded Midnight and headed to the Sale Barn. Only Larry was sorry to see him go, as they had spent many hours at war together.

Daddy only got twenty-five dollars for that black Shetland and a good laugh. As Daddy watched

Scraps of Laughter
for Ladies

across the sale ring, some kids begged their daddy to buy that 'cute' horse! And their daddy did.

Daddy met the man on the way out of the Sale Barn. He shook his hand and told him, "Midnight is what my kids called that horse, but Satan might be a better name for that Black Shetland." He folded the twenty-five dollars and stuck it in his overalls bib pocket, turned, and walked away with a smile.

Scraps of Laughter for Ladies

Greg and I: I Cook, He Eats!

When my husband and I were first married, I loved to try out my cooking skills. Sometimes, they needed help, so I would look at Mama's cookbooks and magazines.

We had only been married a few years when I was thumbing through a Good Housekeeping Magazine, and I stumbled on the recipe section. It was fall, and I found a recipe that had an amazing picture. There was a pile of shiny, red apples with a copper pot of chili, a string of dried chili peppers, and autumn leaves scattered over a picnic table under trees of brilliant foliage. It was a beautiful picture. So…I decided to make that chili. Maybe Greg would like it better. He always poured half a bottle of catsup into my chili. He told me the catsup made it taste like his mom's chili. He had even told me his mother would probably give me her chili recipe if I asked for it. But I didn't want her chili recipe. I wanted him to like my chili!

I looked at the beautiful picture again and sighed. Cook by picture? Why not? That is how I order from the menu in a restaurant. If it looks good, it must be good. I have only gotten burned with that idea once. The picture hadn't shown the hunk of soggy bread beneath fish topped with strips of kale, and I guess I had assumed the fish would be grilled and seasoned. It wasn't, but it had looked good in the picture.

I shook my head to clear that memory. Now for the chili.

I believe this Good Housekeeping chili called for about a half-dozen apples, and I had apples along

97

with the rest of the ingredients. Good Housekeeping and I went into the kitchen to make apple chili.

I browned, diced, measured, and mixed. I stirred, and soon, the blissful fall aroma filled the air. This chili looked about the same as the chili in the picture… minus the trees and picnic table, the pile of apples, the string of red chilis, and scattered leaves. I smiled as it bubbled. Now for the taste test. I dipped a wooden spoon in the pot, scooped chili, and held it to my lips to blow and cool. It smelled heavenly. I breathed in deeply. My mouth was watering. I licked my lips and slid the spoon between them.

"MMM…UH?" There was a chili taste along with a sort of sour-sweet apple taste. It was rather like applesauce and chili mixed together.

I tasted it again. "Ooowee," I shuddered.

I dropped the spoon and grabbed my Good Housekeeping magazine. Something had to be wrong. I went over each ingredient and checked them off one by one. "Hamburger, yes, check…onions, yes, check…chili powder, yes, check…beans, yes, check…garlic, yes, check…tomato sauce, yes, check, and yes…apples, check." Everything was in that chili that was supposed to be there.

I shrugged my shoulders and opened the cabinet doors to look at my spices. I had to have something to help this chili along. There was ginger, turmeric, nutmeg, alum, cinnamon…I shrugged my shoulders. Oh, southwest seasoning…maybe? I opened the lid and shook wildly a couple of times, stirred, and tasted again. "UH?" It didn't help. Below, I yanked my cabinet doors wide. I had potatoes, rice, and zucchini squash. I shook my head. Nothing. I had nothing to make this chili taste as wonderful as the picture looked.

Maybe I could mix up some brownies so the chili would be more acceptable...but I didn't have time for brownies. I heard the front door open.

"Honey, I am home. It sure smells good. MMMM. Maybe chili and apple pie?" Greg popped his head around the corner with a smile. He wrapped his arms around me and bragged, "Not every man gets to come home to chili and apple pie!"

I wish I had thought of apple pie! That half of a dozen apples would have been better received. "Wash up, Honey," I told him as I grabbed the potholders and carried the apple chili, smoking with doom, to the middle of the table.

I will never forget the look on his face as that first spoonful went into his mouth. He chewed, paused, studied deeply into the depths of his bowl, stirred a bit with his spoon, and swallowed. "Oh, no! Honey, did you drop the apple pie into the chili?"

I should have said, "Yes," but I didn't. I just shook my head, "New recipe, highly recommended by Good Housekeeping."

"Oh, Good Housekeeping? You still have that magazine?"

I nodded.

"Trash it, or better yet, give it to me, and I will trash it." Greg laughed as he slowly downed the whole bowl of chili. There was nothing else to eat. He didn't take seconds. With the last swallow, he quietly said, "Hon, you don't need to ever make this chili again. I love how you usually make it."

Scraps of Laughter
for Ladies

I smiled. He loved how I usually made my chili, Not how his mother made chili! And, this time, he hadn't added any catsup!

****

A few years later, Greg had taken his first pastorate. It was a little church in Nebraska, and we were having the time of our lives. We had just had a youth rally out in the Wild Cat Hills. Teens from all over southwestern Nebraska had come. It was a success, but we had a bunch of hot dog buns left; there were no hot dogs, just the buns. The church had no deep freeze, I had no deep freeze, and no one else offered theirs. So, we divvied up the hot dog buns and took them home. For the next few weeks, I used hot dog buns for eggs, bacon, and toast. I used hot dog buns in meatloaf. I used hot dog buns with peanut butter and jelly. We even rolled lunch meat and tucked it in the hot dog buns for sandwiches. Then came the day when one of our members brought us some hamburger. Greg's favorite is a good old hamburger. So, I used hot dog buns for hamburgers.

Carefully, just like a potter, I molded and patted the hamburger to fit the hot dog buns. I shaped them like a hot dog…a long, rolled tube-shaped hamburger. I stuck them in the pan and turned on the heat. As they began to cook, I noticed a subtle change beginning to take place. They no longer looked like rolled hamburgers, but they did not look like hot dogs either. They looked like…well…they looked like something you would find outside on the trail after taking your Rottweiler for a walk! They certainly did not look like something you want to see on your kitchen table! Yet, I could not throw them away. It WAS hamburger, and hamburger cost money. I would just serve it anyway. Besides, it was only Greg, Boone, and me.

For supper, I tucked my hamburger/hot dogs into the buns and placed them on the plates. I thought the buns would hide them a little. Boone was a toddler. He said nothing. Greg grabbed two of them, the catsup, and gasped as he held the bottle in the air over the hotdog bun: "Oh my word! What, in tarnation, is this?" He sat the catsup down and bent his head over the hamburger/hot dog to scrutinize the thing.

"Well, what does it look like?" I asked.

He glared at me, "You know what it looks like! I want to know what it is."

"Smell it," I ordered.

"I am not going to smell that, that… thing until you tell me what it is," he blared.

It was Boone who answered, "Goggie pooh." Boone grabbed his hamburger/hot dog out of its bun and shoved the thing into his mouth.

Greg gagged.

I laughed, "It is not 'goggie pooh.'" I tried to explain what I had done.

Years later, we told all four of our kids about the hot dog/hamburger incident when they were in their teens. They thought it was funny, so Greg and I decided to fix them for supper that night. "You can hear about it, but you have to see it to get the full effect," Greg said as he pulled out the grill. Together, we laughed at the transformation that took place on the grill. Together we both watched our kids as we sat the platter on the table in the midst of our children. Laughter filled the kitchen as the jokes began. Just before prayer, the doorbell rang. Chelle and Jodie

Scraps of Laughter
for Ladies

Sparks were on their way to college and had stopped for the night. We welcomed them, and as always, we loved that surprise, but this time, the surprise was on them.

Our family scooted and squished to make room for Chelle and Jodie with us around the table, and then, as our guests, we passed the hot dog/hamburgers to them first.

Weakly, Chelle held the platter over her plate, lifted her eyes, and asked, "What is this?"

"Doggie pooh. Good stuff. Take two," Boone told her, grabbed one himself, and shoved it in his mouth. His eyes lit as he watched Chelle and Jodie.

Laughter serenaded our supper.

* * * * * * * *

Last Saturday night, after a good hunk of the day traveling, Greg and I were tired. For supper, all I wanted was a small bowl of soup. I like that. Greg thinks soup is just a starter, paving the road for something bigger and better. I had eaten half of a personal pan pizza for lunch, so I gave the rest to him with a big cup of tomato soup…his favorite. With his first bite, he blinked, "This soup kind of tastes like the can."

"Well, it came out of the can," I told him.

"Yes, I know, but it tastes like the can. You know, kind of like Aluminum, aluminummy."

"Really? Let me check the expiration date," I jumped up and headed for the trash. I dug the empty can out and read. "Honey, the date is fine. It has a

Scraps of Laughter
for Ladies

whole year before it expires. But if it tastes funny, don't eat it."

He took another bite and shrugged his shoulders, "Oh, I guess it's not so bad."

I shook my head. Men.

When he was down to the last drop, he held up a spoon load of tomato soup. Casually, he asked, "Honey, what is this?"

I looked. Hanging from his spoon drooped a long, jelly-clear stringy mass with a couple of black dots at each end. It appeared to be an emaciated earthworm...dangling in a soupy spoon grave.

Silence settled between Greg and me. That floaty-gurgling feeling clasped and rolled my stomach into a knot. I took a deep breath and seized a thought. "The pizza. Honey. Did you dip the pizza in your soup?"

"Well, Yes. That is what you do. You dip your sandwich in tomato soup, only it was pizza instead."

"Yes!" I was relieved, "It is not a worm! It must be an onion off the pizza!"

Greg studied the spoon with the soup and the dangling, questionable onion that sure looked like a worm. He raised his eyebrows. "Hmmm, could be. Over the lips and over the gums, watch out, tummy, here it comes!" Then he shoved it into his mouth, chomped, and swallowed.

"Yuck," I gaged.

He laughed, "You know John the Baptist ate locusts!"

I shook my head. Men. Okay, if John the Baptist could do it...why not my husband?

AND...

Scraps of Laughter
for Ladies

It was over a week ago, and Greg is still alive and kicking!

I guess that is how our marriage works: I cook, he eats!

Scraps of Laughter
for Ladies

Visitation

We have a preacher friend who named his horse Visitation. When someone would call for him, and he was out riding, the person who answered the phone was instructed to say the Pastor was on Visitation.

Visitation. So many things have happened on visitation. I have been bitten by dogs, chased by dogs, and slapped at by cats. Once, Clay dove on top of the van because of a pit bull; while I pretended, I was not afraid and prayed. There was no way anyone was going to see me try to climb a van. I have had a big man answer the door with an even bigger butcher knife in hand, and I've had a man call me to come on in without a single stitch of clothing.

Yet visitation is a very important part of the ministry. We have had the privilege of leading people to the Lord, gathering bus children, and adding to the church.

In Amarillo, we had visitation every Saturday morning at 10:00 o'clock. We always took our kids, but to sweeten the pot, we would go to the cheap pop store for a soda of choice. As the years passed, everyone left the church for visitation with cards in hand and met at the cheap pop store. Now, this store was not in the best part of Amarillo, so I was glad of the company.

Our youngest daughter will not let me forget the time she and I were partners. As we were leaving the cheap pop store, an old lady with her belongings piled high on a Walmart cart, wheeled into the parking lot. She sagged beneath three or four layers of clothes. Wildly splayed, grey hair splashed from beneath her battered felt hat. A black-knitted glove and a big brown leather glove kept her hands warm even though it was a hot spring day.

I pulled the church van to a halt. "Kelloway, jump out and give this tract to that lady." I shoved a couple of dollars into the folds of the tract and placed it into Kelloway's hand.

"Mom," she whined. "Why?"

I blinked. "Because I'm your mom, and she needs to know about Jesus. It won't take but a minute."

Kelloway rolled her middle school eyes, opened the door, and ran to the cart lady.

I watched. That old lady pointed her gloved finger at my daughter and shook it while parting words of wisdom to her.

Kelloway backed away as the lecture continued. She jumped into the van and slammed the door. "I never want to do that again," she huffed and glared. "That lady is crazy."

"Crazy or not, she still needs the Lord," I told her.

Kelloway's eyes grew big. "Crazy, Mom? Maybe you better be the one to talk to her next time. You will have more in common."

I shook my head and asked, "What did she tell you?"

"Mom, she told me that if I go to a Catholic school and eat their lunches, I will get pregnant." Kelloway drew her eyebrows together, "Mom, I told her I wasn't Catholic, but she didn't care. She just kept telling me I was going to get pregnant if I ate their food. Mom. She is crazy. Please don't ever make me do that again," she begged.

Scraps of Laughter
for Ladies

I laughed, but from that day on, we both noted the crazy cart lady, and Kelloway ducked when we would pass so she wouldn't see her, point at her and shout about being pregnant from Catholic school food. A few years later the crazy cart Lady died, and the Amarillo Globe News ran an article on her. She was believed to have been one of the richest ladies in Amarillo.

A lot of transients roamed the streets around our cheap pop store. One Saturday morning, I pulled the church van in the parking lot with my visiting sister, Cathy, as my partner. Now, my sister is from a little rural farm in Kansas. She is not used to our 'hood' as we call our neighborhood. We went into the store, got our cheap sodas, and on the way out, we noticed a homeless man approaching. He was much bigger and hairier than Cathy and I put together, plus he wore gang apparel that displayed his multi-tattooed arms, neck and chest (Where it wasn't hairy.) Really, it was unique. He had shaved the face and trunk of the Mammoth tattooed on his chest and let the rest of the mammoth grow hair.

Cathy's eyes flew open, and her fingers became a tight knot about her purse, "Sandy, I think he is going to mug us."

I sighed, "No, he'll probably just ask for money. It's the church name on the side of the van. They know we'll give them something. It's okay. I'll give him a pack of crackers," I told her.

She frowned and looked at me with a question. "A pack of crackers?"

I explained, "My husband made me promise to never give money. He says they will take that money and buy alcohol or drugs; thus, you are supporting their habit. So, I know Greg keeps packages of peanut butter crackers in all our vehicles, and I don't mind giving those to anyone who crosses my path." In silence, I looked up through the heavens and mumbled, "Sorry about giving money to the cart lady, Lord."

Cathy picked up her step, "You better get those crackers now, because he's almost here."

I looked, and she was right. I sped up to get to the van first. I hit the button to open the door, but in my hurry, I hit the panic button instead of the unlock button. The horn blared!

My sister, Cathy, was in front of the van. That horn blasted, and Cathy screamed, throwing her arms wide, torpedoing her soda through the air like a grenade. It exploded, showering the parking lot with sticky stuff.

I doubled over laughing.

Cathy laughed after a while.

But…The transient was gone!

And…thereafter, my sister chose not to visit on visitation days.

One Saturday, Tandolynn happened to be the lucky one with me on visitation when we got the news that one of our ladies with diabetes had just become a double amputee. I was telling her all about the operation when I pulled into the cheap pop store, put on the breaks, and switched off the key.

"Stumpy's!" Tandolynn blurted out.

I whipped my head in her direction, "Young Lady, you will not call her Stumpy! That is very disrespectful. Do you understand?"

"But, Mom…" she tried to talk.

Scraps of Laughter
for Ladies

"There are no buts about it. You will not be calling her any names, least of all, Stumpys!" I know my eyes held fire.

Quietly, she pointed across the road. An old bar had opened, and the name adorning the place was 'Stumpy's.'

I raised my eyebrows, "Stumpy's, uh?"

Together, we laughed, and we still laugh about the incident.

One of the times I remember the most was the Saturday we divided into groups, prayed, and left the church headed for the cheap pop store. How Tom and DeeDee beat us there I will never know. I didn't think Tom could bring himself to speed. But as we pulled in, Tom and DeeDee were already in their car, pops in hand, and ready to back out of their parking spot. Greg stopped the van to wait for their space.

I laughed. "Watch this!" I told my husband. I jumped out, leaving the door swinging wide, and ran to the passenger side of the car, where DeeDee sat unaware.

I smashed my face and spread my hands against her window in Garfield style, and slid from the top of the window to the bottom, dragging my tongue, stringing spit.

DeeDee yelled, and I backed away laughing. Then I noticed Tom flinging open his door wildly. He stepped to his full height and glared at me over the top of the car. I blinked and swallowed. That was not Tom, and this man was mad. I bent down and peered in the window at DeeDee. She was not my friend DeeDee. She was a terrified stranger with eyes popping out of her head, fingers pressed through the styrofoam of her cup, and coke spraying out the finger holes.

Scraps of Laughter
for Ladies

I backed away from the vehicle, spreading my hands wide, "I am so sorry. I thought you were my friends, Tom and DeeDee!"

"That's how you treat your friends?" The man glared and asked in disbelief.

I shrugged and repeated how sorry I was, and believe me, I was sorry now.

My husband came to my rescue. He walked up and put his protective arm around me, "I think she's going through menopause," he explained, "you know, the change of life in a woman that affects everyone in their pathway."

The man raised his eyebrows in a knowing look and nodded.

My husband patted my arm, "We are trying to get through it without medication."

I swung my head toward him and opened my mouth.

He shushed me! He smashed his finger on my lips and shushed me! "Now, Honey, remember it is better not to say anything than to say something you will regret."

I know sparks were jumping from my eyes, but he firmly kept his arm around me and held me close and tight.

All I could think of was when I got back into the van…and I know my eyes wandered there.

So did the man's, "That's a church van?"

My husband answered, "It sure is, and I am the Pastor." He whipped a tract out of his pocket, "We would love to have you come and visit, and would you please let me buy your wife another soda?"

When we climbed into the van to leave, my husband turned to me, "Now that was a new approach,

Honey. I think it might work. He seemed to think they would come visit our services to see what we have to offer." He paused, nibbling his bottom lip, "But next time, Honey, when you jump out of the van, I would appreciate you telling me your plans so I can be better prepared."

I glared, "You know I thought it was Tom and DeeDee!"

He laughed.

"And menopause? Menopause without medication?" I fumed.

Tears rolled out of his eyes.

"And if you ever try to shush me like that again, I will bite your finger off!" I seethed.

My husband was laughing so hard he didn't dare put the van in gear. Finally, he drew in a gulp of air to steady himself, "I saw that streak of…" he paused, searching for the right word.

I finished for him, "Anger? Vengeance?"

He wiped his eyes, "You know when I tell this from the pulpit, I'll bet we have a bunch of people on visitation. They will all want to be your partner."

"You wouldn't."

"You'll never know, Hon, because you'll be in Jr. Church."

I rolled my eyes and shook my head. "Visitation." I hope all have as much fun on visitation as my husband seemed to have on visitation!

Scraps of Laughter
for Ladies

Dishwater Blonde

For most of my grade school years, I went to a little country school. Now, don't age me yet! Not all the classes were in one room. There were two classes taught in each room, 1st and 2nd, 3rd and 4th, 5th and 6th, and 7th and 8th. My class was one of the biggest. We had fourteen: eight boys and six girls. Each year you went to school, you knew exactly who was going to be in your class and who was going to be your teacher. You really hoped you liked your teacher because you were stuck with the same one for two years straight. There were certain things that you knew starting from first grade going clear through eighth grade. They were things like Cheryl Soles was in love with Harold Knoll, and when they were old enough, they were going to get married. Patrick Miller had to take second grade over again, and Judy Hawk always got the smartest kid award at the end of the year. But the important things happened on the playground. I could high jump higher than everyone in my class except for Donald Knoll. I could broad jump further than everyone in my class except for Donald Knoll. I could run faster than everyone in my class except for Donald Knoll, and sometimes, I just let him win. I had such a crush on him, and he had such a crush on me that we couldn't even speak to each other. He would send Ronald Liker to tell Judy Hawk to tell me that he liked me. In return, I would have Judy Hawk go tell Ronald Liker that I liked him, too. Those were things that never changed from the time we started grade school until we finished. However, one year that I remember so vividly with pain was the year I found

Scraps of Laughter
for Ladies

out I was a dishwater blonde.

Just before Christmas, parts were handed out for our school play. I was given the part of an old rag doll in a toy shop that no one bought for Christmas. On Christmas Eve the old rag doll was miraculously turned into a beautiful angel on top of the big Christmas tree in the town square. Judy Hawk was the angel. I didn't think much about it until Robert Dixon taunted me on the playground.

It had snowed, and it was cold. Mr. Hale had given us a choice of playing in the gym or braving the outside world. All the boys went out, leaving the gym for the "sissy" girls. Since there was no way that I was going to ever be a "sissy" girl, I talked Judy Hawk into bundling up and coming out with me. Big mistake! The playground game was snowball war, and Judy and I were outnumbered. She wanted to retreat to the gym, but not me. I packed a huge hunk of snow, hurled it at the closest target, and got a bull's eye. It went right down the neck of Robert Dixon's parka. With disgust and a few choice fighting words, Robert Dixon began scooping snow from the inside of his coat. All the other boys started laughing at him 'cause he had gotten bombed by a girl. He glared at me. "You know why you got the part of a rag doll instead of the angel in the Christmas program? I'll tell you why! It's 'cause you look like a rag doll. You got rag doll hair! Yuk hair! Dishwater blonde hair!"

In a flash, I was in front of him, "Take it back!"

"Make me!" he sneered.

I punched him in the gut, dropped him to the ground, and rubbed his face in the snow.

Everyone thought it was funny except Robert Dixon, Robert Dixon's mother, and my mother.

Scraps of Laughter
for Ladies

That was Friday. Saturday, Mom had a long talk with me. She was washing my hair, and while it was all suds up, she began, "I heard that you and Robert Dixon had a disagreement."

I didn't say anything. I'm not sure, but I don't think I was even breathing. That's how most of our talks went anyway. She talked. I listened.

"Is it true that you punched Robert in the stomach and rubbed his face in the snow?"

I blinked, licked my lips, and nodded.

"Young ladies don't punch, and they certainly don't rub someone's face in the snow," she explained.

I wiped a sudsy hunk of hair away from my eye, "But . . ."

"No buts about it," she interrupted me. "You will pull Robert Dixon aside on Monday, and you will apologize. Am I understood?" Mom didn't leave any room for argument, so I nodded.

After a few quiet moments, I asked, "Mom, what color is my hair?"

"Mmmm," she paused, "well, I would say it's dishwater blonde."

My heart stopped. My own Mother had called me exactly what I had punched Robert Dixon for! "Dishwater blonde? What does that mean?"

"It means that your hair is kind of between blonde and brown, sort of dirty blonde like dishwater," she colored the picture for me.

I swallowed. Dishwater blonde. Wow! That rated right up there with gag green and puke yellow! It felt like one of those invisible rocks had hit me in the eyes, sank to the bottom of my stomach, and wedged there. And that explained why I had heard Mom say so many times that she was glad my sister, Cathy, had

Scraps of Laughter
for Ladies

deep dark hair like her father. I never, ever heard her say she was glad I was a dishwater blonde! Why, I didn't even know what I was until then! And I probably did get the rag doll part because of my hair! After all, Judy's hair always hung in nice little ringlets. Mine did whatever it wanted to do when it wanted to do it. That probably went with this dishwater blonde stuff, too! Judy Hawk had angel hair. I had rag doll, dishwater blonde stuff!

When my hair was dry, I locked myself in the bathroom and stood in front of the mirror. I studied my hair. No way was I going to settle for being a dishwater blonde. It was the color of ripened wheat, so that's what I would be: ripened wheat!

Monday morning, Mom reminded me that I was to apologize. to Robert Dixon (Like I could forget!)

At recess, I waited until Robert Dixon was alone, then I told him through clenched teeth, "I need to talk to you!"

His eyes got wild, and he took out running. I belted out after him and caught up with him just before he could run into the school. I grabbed the collar of his coat and slammed him against the brick building. "My Mother told me to tell you this. 'Sorry!' And this (I grabbed a hunk of my hair and shoved it in his face) is not dishwater blonde! It is ripened wheat!" I dropped hold of his coat collar, turned, spit on the ground, and stomped away.

That should have been the end of it, but it wasn't. I would find Ivory dishwashing ads and coupons on my desk. Once, there was even an empty bottle of the stuff in my coat pocket. But the worst came one day as we filed into lunch. Girls sat on one side of the table, and boys on the other. I ended up

Scraps of Laughter
for Ladies

right across the table from Donald Knoll. My heart pounded. It was hard to concentrate on eating, and it didn't make it any easier that everyone began teasing us about liking each other. We were both handling it well until someone said something funny. I had a mouthful of milk. I clamped my lips shut. There was no way that I wanted to drool milk down my chin in front of Donald Knoll. But I couldn't swallow, and I couldn't stop laughing. Something had to give. It did. To my horror, milk shot out my nose, across the table, and landed in Donald Knoll's chocolate pudding. In the tiny pause that followed, Robert Dixon gloated, "Hey! She even squirts like a bottle of Ivory dishwashing liquid!" Our table laughed so hard that we all had to set out recess and do extra math facts. And, to my horror, I was branded with the new nickname of Ivory Squirts!

For our church Christmas program that year, Mom made me the most adorable pink and white checked dress. It was so pretty that I felt beautiful in it, even for a ripened wheat blonde! I wore it with pride for our church Christmas program, and that's when the thought hit me. If I wore this wonderful dress to school, everyone would see how beautiful I was, and no one would dare call me Ivory Squirts anymore.

I begged and pleaded with Mom until she gave in. She probably thought it would make me act like a lady.

Monday morning, I flounced into the classroom with ruffles swirling. I felt grand. Nothing could bother me today.

We had an especially warm day for December, so everyone pulled their coats off and dropped them on the winter playground at recess. I was busy swinging higher than anyone else when Robert Dixon ran by. He cupped his hands around his mouth and shouted, "Ivory Squirts!"

Beautiful dress or not, this ripened wheat blonde was going to make him eat dirt! I dove out of that swing and landed on my feet. Only…my dress stayed in the swing. It had caught in the chains and ripped right off my body! Yet, it was beautiful. The swing was waltzing through the air, waving long strands of pink and white checkered ruffles. It was like a parade or a party until I realized the decorations were my dress, my beautiful Christmas dress!

Then the bomb hit me. If that was my dress, I was standing on the playground in my underwear! I gasped.

Robert Dixon screeched out a wolf whistle, and everyone laughed, sounding like a drum roll.

I ran all the way home in my underwear without anyone's permission.

The night of our Christmas program finally arrived, and I played the part of the rag doll with ripened wheat hair well. But never will I be able to explain the feeling that welled up inside of me as the curtain parted on the last scene. In the middle of Town Square was the magnificent Christmas tree with the pretty Judy Hawk angel on top. Tied to each branch fluttered strips of pink and white checked material which was: MY CHRISTMAS DRESS!

Robert Dixon was going to die!

Scraps of Laughter for Ladies

Shoulder Pads

So, it was going to be one of those days. I closed my eyes and shoved my face back under the steaming shower head. I had just shaved my legs with the razor closed. Oh, well! Quickly, I repeated the ordeal. I dried and dressed and stood in front of the mirror. Something was missing. I turned to the side, then back to the front. That was it! My shoulders slope something awful, and it is very unglamorous. So, I have these molded shoulder pads. You sit them on your shoulders underneath your clothes, and voila! Nice square shoulders! I went to my dresser drawer and pulled them out. Now, my shoulder pads are old and have been used a lot. I need new ones, but I can't find them anywhere and believe me, I have tried! I went to the mirror and popped them in place. Yes, that looked much better.

At work, this problem developed. My shoulder pads would not stay in place. I was busy typing when a friend walked by. She passed my desk. She stopped, backed up, and leaned close to me. "You been working out?" she asked.

I smiled and thought, "Thanks to these shoulder pads, I look slimmer!" I told her, "No, I have not been working out. Why?" I asked, hoping for a compliment.

"Well," her eyes sparkled as she reached over and thumped my arm, "That is quite a bicep!"

I looked down and groaned. My shoulder pads had slipped down into the sleeves of my blouse, and I certainly did have tremendous biceps. My friend laughed, and I told her to go away. She giggled and threw over her shoulder, "You want to get together for

119

Scraps of Laughter
for Ladies

lunch?"

"Sure," I laughed and began digging in my drawer for safety pins, but I didn't come up with any. However, I did find a couple of straight pins. I held them in my hand, rolled them about, and studied them. "I bet I could make them work," I thought.

In the bathroom, I dug the shoulder pad biceps out of my sleeves and arranged them on my shoulders where they should be. Then, I pushed the straight pins in so they could not be seen from the outside. I wiggled around to try them out, and sure enough, they stayed right where they were supposed to.

As I was working away that afternoon, my boss came up behind me. Now I have a very nice boss, but he is always playing pranks on me. He decided to scare me when he saw that I hadn't noticed him because of how diligently I was working. He tip-toed up behind me and grabbed my shoulders. Then he yelled.

I whirled around in my chair.

He was flapping his hand like a chicken that had just lost its head. "What in tarnation do you have on?!" He shoved his thumb into his mouth and began sucking.

"What?" I asked, amazed at seeing my boss suck his thumb.

He yanked his thumb out of his mouth and pushed it toward me. "This! Just look at this!" he wailed.

I began to giggle. He had jammed his thumb into the straight pin, which was holding my shoulder pad in place.

"I don't see the humor," he said. "What happened anyway?"

"It's a long story, and I have to get back to

work," I told him because there was no way that I wanted to explain. Maybe," I winked at him, "you had better watch who you sneak up behind."

After work, I stopped by the grocery store to pick up a few things. I got into the store, grabbed a cart, and headed for the vegetable aisle. Just as I passed the onions, I saw the greeting cards. I needed one. I looked over my shoulder to back up my cart and noticed my shoulder pad was gone! Quickly, I slipped down an empty aisle and began digging in my blouse to see if my shoulder pad was there. Nothing. I looked around. No one was in sight, so I pulled my blouse out and looked down for my shoulder pad. Still nothing! When I looked up, to my horror, there stood a sack boy. Guilt washed over me. He probably thought I was shoplifting! I couldn't think of anything to say. So I blurted out, "Hot in here! Really hot!"

He looked at me strangely and nodded. I put my cart in gear and shoved off. I had to find that shoulder pad. After all, I didn't know if I'd ever be able to buy them again. I started going up and down all the aisles I had been on. Then, I noticed that the sack boy was following me, not so as I would notice, but he was definitely following me! I began to sweat. What if he really did think I was shoplifting? What if they stopped me at the counter and asked if I had put anything in my blouse? What if they wanted to strip-search?! My heart began pounding. What if I had to call my husband and say, "Honey, I'm at the police station. They think I have been shoplifting. Could you come to bail me out?"

I didn't know what to do. I began throwing things into my cart. "Maybe," I reasoned, "if they see how much I am paying for, they will think the sack

121

boy is crazy for even thinking I would shoplift!"

Finally, I went to the checkout counter. There was nowhere else to go. I began unloading my cart. Then I pulled out my checkbook. My hands were clammy. It seemed like it was taking the checker forever, and every now and then, she snuck a strange look at me. Maybe she wondered why I had bought fly paper and oysters. I licked my lips and silently prayed, "Please, Lord. Please, Lord. Please, Lord! Let me get out of this store!"

When she finally rang up the total, I was shaking. I handed her the check.

"Thank you," she smiled and again looked strangely at me. "Would you like a sack boy?" she asked.

"No!" I violently shook my head, "I've been working out!"

"Okay," she handed me the receipt.

I walked out the door. No alarms went off. I breathed a sigh of relief and practically ran to my car. I opened the door and threw the bags in.

I heard steps behind me. I turned. It was the sack boy. "Excuse me, mam," he said, "the manager would like to speak with you."

I froze. I didn't know what to say.

"If you'll just follow me," he waited for me to follow.

I followed. I kept thinking that maybe I should just say I didn't do whatever it was that they thought I might have done! But…nothing would come out.

When we reached the manager's door, the sack boy pulled it open and stepped aside so I could enter. The manager was at his desk. He laid down his pen and stood. "I'm Arnold Black," he said, reaching his hand out to shake mine.

I swallowed, trying to remember my name, but he already knew it.

"Mrs. Waggoner, please have a seat."

I sat.

He took a deep breath, "Mrs. Waggoner, this is a rather uncomfortable situation..."

My eyes went wide. I sure was feeling uncomfortable!

The manager continued, "My sack boy brought this to my attention. He wasn't sure how to handle the situation, but it seems that while you were on aisle three...."

I gritted my teeth and prayed to myself. "Help my husband to understand. PLEASE!"

"Are you alright, Mrs. Waggoner?" the manager paused.

I nodded my head in a lie. How could anyone be alright in this situation?

"When you were on aisle three, my sack boy saw this... fall out of your blouse," He opened his desk drawer and pulled out my molded shoulder pad.

"Oh, my shoulder pad!" I giggled hysterically. Then I tried to explain, "I have the mate right here." I reached into my blouse for the other pad. It was gone! "Oh, no! I lost it!" I moaned.

The manager swallowed and smiled, "Oh, Mrs. Waggoner, I don't think you lost it."

"What?" I asked.

"It's undoubtedly closer than you think," his eyes twinkled.

I looked down. There, in the front of my blouse, was my other shoulder pad all knotted up. I was three across where I should only be two! My face turned red, and I smiled a great happy smile.

"Mrs. Waggoner, we appreciate your business," the manager again reached out to shake my hand.

I shook his hand, the sack boy's hand, and headed to my car. I scooted into my seat and dropped my head on the steering wheel. The horn blew! I looked up, and there stood the sack boy! I waved, stuck the key in the ignition, and threw the car into reverse. Never, never, never, ever, would I enter that store again! And as for those shoulder pads? As soon as I was in traffic, I threw them out the window. In the rear-view mirror, I watched them hit the windshield of the pick-up behind me. It swerved and screeched to the side of the road. I yanked my steering wheel, skidded around the corner, and out of sight. My heart had finally slowed to a regular rhythm as I pulled into my drive. I sat and took a deep breath.

Behind me, a pick-up tooted its horn as it blocked me in my driveway. In the rear-view mirror, I watched as Henry, one of our older deacons, stepped out of his pick-up and strutted to my open window. "Mrs. Pastor, a ways back ya lost these fluffy things out of yer winder. They hit my windshield. I almost wrecked the pick-up, but I saved the fluffy things fer ya."

Bless his heart, he was as proud as a peacock until his wife, Mable, tromped up beside him. "Get yerself back in the pick-up, Henry. I'll take care of this." Mable turned to me with a freezing glare. "Missy, my man don't know what those things are, but I know falsies when I see them. I'll be explaining this to Henry, and I expect he'll be bringing it up to the deacon board, so you best be preparing that preacher husband of yorn." With that she turned and stomped

Scraps of Laughter
for Ladies

toward the pick-up.

I tumbled out of my car and sputtered, "But…but…but they are not falsies! They are molded shoulder pads!"

Mable didn't even turn to look at me. She just yelled over her shoulder, "I know what I saw! And them is falsies!"

"Thank you, Mable!" I threw my hands in the air. What a day. I guess I had best prepare my husband for the next deacon's meeting. I would have to give him my shoulder pads to display, and maybe, just maybe, the deacons would believe him. I smiled and hoped someone would take a picture! And…I sighed…at least he didn't have to bail me out of jail!

But he may have to bail me out at the deacon's meeting.

Scraps of Laughter
for Ladies

Men and Women Don't Think Alike

Men and women don't think alike. Now that isn't something you just know naturally…it's something you learn. I was a slow learner. I didn't even learn it until marriage, and then it took a bit to catch on. I think it was on our honeymoon I began notice an extreme difference in thinking. We got married three weeks after Christmas. That means we shared our first Christmas shortly before we said, "I do." Greg is a cowboy. He comes from a cowboy family. He loves horses and everything that goes with them. My family had a Shetland once, and I sure didn't learn to love horses. I learned to steer clear and run. That Shetland had the meanest temper, the hardest teeth, and he smiled when he bit. Anyway, for Christmas I bought the love of my life a deep chocolate brown cowboy hat. I just knew he would love it, and he did.

On our honeymoon we traveled to the north country of Nebraska and Wyoming. In Cheyenne we found a cozy little park where snowflakes lazily floated in the sunshine. It was as beautiful as our love… Until I packed a snowball and tossed it at my husband. It smashed on his hat. That was how I learned, "You don't mess with a cowboy's hat!" He yelled that at me. I remember blinking and puzzling over the idea. Not only was he serious, but he was down-right mad. And…it made sense to him.

That was our first argument. Just think…I had bought the stupid hat. I had not thrown the snowball hard. The snowball had not dented his hat or knocked it off his head. Just what was the problem?

Scraps of Laughter
for Ladies

"You don't mess with a cowboy's hat!" That was all he would say.

Twenty years later I fumed as the idea struck me. I was not even aiming for his hat in the first place! I know I wasn't because I never hit anything I aim at. I must have been aiming for his guts! So, it had to have been his fault because he must have ducked. Do you know in all these twenty-some years he has never asked me if I aimed the snowball at his hat? And he probably never asked because then he would know it would have been his fault! See…that is how a man thinks.

There is this Christian scientist guy, at the moment, I can't remember his name. Anyway, his theory states that when babies are carried in their mother's womb, during a certain month a male child's brain is washed with a chemical. This chemical kills half of the brain. Now, I tend to agree with this theory. In fact, as far as I am concerned, it may be well over half of the brain. And I am convinced that from there after the 'washing of the brain' males have an adverse reaction to any form of washing. Oh, they like to wash cars because it makes them run faster. But things like hands and feet? That is a different story.

Take teeth. You show them a toothbrush in the morning and that is enough to last them the entire day. If you are lucky, they might get brushed twice on Sundays.

My husband's mom brought him a new toothbrush the last time she came. I took the old one. A few days later my husband asked, "Hun, where is my toothbrush?"

I looked at him. "There," I pointed to the toothbrush holder.

Scraps of Laughter
for Ladies

"Not that one. I want my old toothbrush."

"Why?" I asked, "Your mom brought you that new one."

He groaned, "I know that, but my teeth are used to the old one, Scruffy Blue."

I just looked at him. "You name your toothbrushes?"

"You don't?"

I shook my head.

"Well, where is it? You didn't throw it away, did you?" he began to panic.

I shook my head and began to worry how I was going to tell him his toothbrush had become my household tool.

"Well?" he demanded.

I hesitated gently thinking how I could answer.

"Just tell me," he ordered.

I shrugged, "In the bottom drawer."

He yanked open that drawer and began digging. "Yes! Scruffy Blue!" He gloated as he held up his old toothbrush with a smile of victory.

I should have just let him use it without saying a word, but he is my husband of many years. What if he got sick and died? So, I latched onto his toothbrush fist and confessed. "Honey, I used your old, toothbrush, Scruffy Blue, to clean with."

He looked devastated, so I suggested. "Listen, if you dip it in Clorox, it will probably kill all the germs."

"Clorox?!" he yelled. "Clorox? You want to kill me?"

"No," I gasped. "I want to kill the germs."

He rolled Scruffy Blue in his hand for a moment. "Just what did you clean with it?"

Scraps of Laughter
for Ladies

I bit my lower lip. "The sink. The groady stuff around the faucet."

His eyes dropped to the sink. "Oh," he shrugged, "That ain't bad."

"Well, it's not bad now. You should have seen it before I cleaned it." I shook my head. It was just like a man to have never noticed it was dirty in the first place.

"No," he threw over his shoulder, "I mean it ain't bad like if you had cleaned the commode with it. Now, that would have ruined Scruffy Blue, but just a little sink crud? I'm a man, and I can handle that."

He pulled the top drawer open, grabbed the toothpaste, and laid it on thick. "Besides, toothpaste will kill anything." He shoved the toothbrush in his mouth and scrubbed.

I vowed never to drink after him again. I left the bathroom and headed downstairs. I had a lot on my mind. Boys. My boys. I wondered if there was any hope for them.

At the bottom of the stairs, ten-year-old Clay came barging in from the back yard. He was filthy.

"What have you been doing, Son?" I asked.

"Playin'."

"What?"

"I was Batman and Buster was the Joker, and we was wrestling, and I beat him up!" Clay smiled proudly.

"You beat up your dog?"

"Ah, Mom, he was the Joker!"

"Poor Buster," I shook my head.

"Poor Buster? Mom. Buster barfed on my back!" Clay didn't feel the least bit sorry for his dog.

"Yuk," I turned him around. "Go take a bath."

Scraps of Laughter
for Ladies

"In the middle of the day?"

"Yes."

"But, Mom, it's Saturday. I don't need a bath 'til nighttime," he protested.

"Clay, your shirt…"

"So," he looked blank. "I'll just change shirts, big deal."

"It's in your hair, Son."

He shrugged. "Mom, Buster licked most of it off, and I'll wipe out the rest with the shirt."

"No. you won't. You'll march into that bathroom this minute and run bath water," I ordered.

He groaned again. "Some Saturday! I'm probably the only boy around that has to start Saturday with a bath."

"And probably end it with a bath." I warned him, "Poor abused boy. To the tub, Young Man." I stood firm.

He turned and drudged slowly to the bathroom.

"While you are there, brush your teeth," I called after him.

"Mom, I haven't even eaten very much today." He held his hands wide.

"Brush them," I shook my head. Defiantly his brain had been washed with some chemical, but not any chemical found in cleaning solutions.

While I stood there thinking, my husband came up behind me.

"Making that poor boy take a bath on Saturday morning?"

"And probably again on Saturday night," I sighed.

"Poor boy. Every day you remind me more of my mother," he gazed at the closed bathroom door.

Scraps of Laughter
for Ladies

"Oh?" His mother? Now don't get me wrong. She is a nice lady, but what wife wants to remind her husband of his mother? My blood began to boil. Slowly, I calmed down and gasped.

"What?" my husband turned to me.

"Oh, nothing," I whispered.

"Yes, there is. I can tell by the look on your face. Tell me what's the matter," he begged.

"Nothing…" I let it dangle in the air like bait.

"Yes, there is. Now, tell me what it is," he ordered.

"Something. Nothing much. Just something that I remembered. It's really nothing, Honey." Weakly, I smiled.

"Nothing? Then tell me," he said.

"Okay, but only because you insist," slowly, I swallowed.

"Yes…" he waited.

I bit my lower lip. "I just remembered, Honey, I used your old toothbrush, Scrubby Blue, on Buster's teeth before I took him to the vet a couple of days ago. Then in the car Buster got sick and barfed on the floor mat. I couldn't get the barf out of the grooves, so I used Scrubby Blue. Honey, I am so sorry."

My husband turned white, dropped his head and ran to the closest bathroom.

"Hey," Clay yelled as his privacy was invaded, "I'm taking a bath…"

Like a volcano, my husband exploded, and Clay choked, "Yuk! You and Buster!"

I smiled. So, I remind my husband of his mother? Later I would tell him it wasn't true…maybe.

Scraps of Laughter
for Ladies

The Girdle

Two of the kids are off to school. The other two are still sleeping. I love that small portion of day when there is a pinch of quiet time. It is also my thinking time. As I sat gazing out of the Kitchen window over a cup of hot chocolate, Natalie rounded the corner of her house. She was hauling a coiled hose over her shoulder and stringing it out. I worry about Natalie. She is much too thin especially considering the fact she is five months pregnant. Why, she has been in maternity clothes for only a couple of weeks and even so, she is hardly showing at all, and if you ask me....THAT IS NOT HEALTHY!!! Of course I am not an expert on the matter, but I have had four kids. And I have always shown by at least six weeks. I guess some of us just carry differently.

It was that incident which put me to remembering. A couple of months back I took cookies to Tandolynn's birthday party at school. A little boy ran up and hugged me. Slowly he backed away from me, shoved his hands in his pockets with wonder and said, "Hey, Tandolynn, you didn't tell me your mama was going to have a baby!"

With sparkles in her eyes Tandolynn dropped her mouth open and her eyes to my tummy, "A baby!" Then she began dancing, "A baby! A Baby! Oh, boy, Mama's going to have a baby!"

"No!" I pushed my hand on top of her bouncing pigtails to stop her jumping and turned her head toward my eyes, "No baby. This is just a small pooch left over from having babies, kind of like a kangaroo

133

keeps her pouch even though she doesn't have a baby kangaroo anymore."

The little boy's eyes widened and dropped to my stomach, "Your mama has a kangaroo pouch? That's really cool and scary!"

Tandolynn tilted her head to one side and squinted at me.

The teacher came to my rescue, "Everyone say thank you to Tandolynn's mama for the cookies and kool-aid." As she walked me to the door heralded by thank yous she smiled and shook her head, "Kids say the strangest things."

"Yes, they do don't they," I smiled and thought I had a few strange things I would like to say back…but they are kids, so I didn't."

Kids! As I tried to bounce back to the present I remembered our family reunion when cute little Henrietta had skipped over to me and asked, "Aunt Sandy?"

I smiled down at the little angelic face, "Yes, Dear?"

"My mommy wants to know if you are P. G. again."

I plastered a smile on my face and looked across the room to where little Henrietta's mommy sat. She sweetly smiled and waved.

Henrietta tugged on my shirt tail, "Well, are you?"

I shook my head and said, "Tell your mommy that it is a low goiter, and we haven't decided what to do with it yet."

"Okay," she skipped off toward her mother.

Boy! The nerve of some people!

Scraps of Laughter
for Ladies

My doorbell rang crashing me to the present again. It was the postman with a package.

"Morning to you, Mrs. Waggoner. Fine day isn't it?"

"It surely is. How are you doing?" I asked.

"Just pretty fine, and it looks like you are, too!"

"Huh?" I questioned.

He patted his stomach, "It must be in the water around here. You're the third one on this block who is in the family way. Congratulations, Mrs. Waggoner!" With a wink and a tip of the hat he turned and walked away whistling.

"What?"

Slowly I closed the door and leaned against it. I looked down at my tummy. With a deep breath I tried to suck it in. Gallantly I moved through the living room and to the bathroom mirror for a sideways angle. Yep. They were right. Even sucked in I looked three to four months along. I shook my head and tried to think back to my high school P.E. class and those painful tummy tighteners. Too bad I hadn't paid much attention then as it would have come in handy now.

I went to the living room and grabbed the paper looking for the T.V. guide. "Somewhere," I muttered, "there is this Hawaiian guy with an exercise program. Maybe, just maybe I would try that. While flipping through the paper I found a sale bill. "Lingerie, 50% sale! Only Friday and Saturday!" it read in bold, black letters.

"That's it!" excitedly I thumped the paper. "That's my answer to quick weight loss! I'll bet one of those girdle things would make me look at least ten pounds lighter!"

Scraps of Laughter for Ladies

Quickly I threw my clothes on and called my friend, Dee Dee. "Dee Dee, I have a small errand to run, if I bring the kids over after I wake them up, could you watch them for a while?"

"Sure, what's up?" she asked.

"Oh, I'll explain later. I've got to hurry. Thanks a bunch! You're one in a million!" I clicked the phone down.

As soon as I had pulled the kids from bed, fed them and dressed them, I stashed them in the car and headed for Dee Dee's. Then I bee-lined to the lingerie sale.

There were a bunch of bargain hunters, and it was easy to see where the lingerie section was. That's where they were! With no fear, I went directly to the mob. The panty and slip isle had quite a few people, the bra section was packed, but the little segment designated for girdles was empty. I slipped into that space and began reading boxes.

"What size?"

I jumped and tried to hide the box behind me.

The sales lady peeked over my shoulder, "I'm sorry. I didn't mean to scare you. I just needed to know what size you wanted."

"Well," I rolled my eyes, "I really don't know. I have never bought one of these before."

"I see," her eyes dropped to my stomach, "a first timer. Why don't you give this one a try." She handed me a box which read, "One size fits all."

"Oh," I shrugged my shoulders. That sounded like a good idea. She turned to help another customer who was waving a bra in the air and asking if it came in purple.

Scraps of Laughter
for Ladies

Quickly I pulled the girdle out of the box. I gasped! One size fits all of what, I wondered. I didn't even think I could get it up over my kneecaps!

The sales lady turned back my way, "It's really wonderfully strong elastic. It is made out of the same rubber plant they use to make Michelin tires." She must have seen the look of horror on my face or read my mind. She took the girdle and hooked it over a protruding rod on the top of a clothing rack and began to pull. "See how well it stretches."

My mouth dropped open in amazement. She had that girdle stretched clear across the aisle.

"And watch this," she said as she thumped the stretched elastic. That elastic sang. "See how firm it is? It is one of our best sellers. Would you like to try it on?"

I paused.

"Would you like me to help you try it on?" she asked.

Violently I shook my head. No one was ever going to see me put that thing on.

She smiled and handed me the girdle and the key to dressing room number three.

I swallowed and nodded a thank you. At the dressing room I eased in and closed the door. There was no lock on the inside, so I shoved the lone chair in front of the door. I wanted no accidental witnesses. With my back to the mirror I slid off my skirt, and the battle began. Both feet went through the leg holes fine, and there wasn't much problem up my calves. Over the knees was a cinch, but then my legs were bound together. I began a series of forward and backward motions all the while pulling and gained maybe an

Scraps of Laughter
for Ladies

inch or two. I was huffing as I realized I needed more effort. I started jumping while pulling.

I was concentrating so hard that when the sales lady rapped on the door to see if I needed help my heart stopped!

"No!" I pushed through clenched teeth. I heard her stand there for a moment before she walked away from my door.

I would have to try a quieter method. I dropped to the floor and swiveled my legs around. I took my hand and tried stuffing handfuls of flesh into the girdle and then pulling. Finally, after tugging, pulling, stuffing and yanking I had that girdle right where it belonged. I lay sprawled in the floor breathing hard. I looked at the ceiling and froze. There was a fire sprinkler! With horror I squinted at it studying it carefully. What if there was a hidden camera? I could just see a video tape submitted to that T.V. funniest home video show! I would die. Quickly I rose and tried to sit in the chair. Sitting was not easy in this girdle! I decided to look ten pounds slimmer wasn't worth this trouble, and I wanted no part of GIRDLES! I started to take it off, but it would not budge! My spare tire had been retreat!

I tried to bend over to pick up my skirt. It did not bend well either. I had to squat down to get my skirt. Slowly I pulled my skirt over my tightly bound body. I would just have to buy this girdle of torture and cut it off when I got home.

I stepped out with the empty box in hand and walked to the clerk. She raised her eyebrows, "An empty box?"

I smiled weakly, "I thought I would wear it home."

Scraps of Laughter
for Ladies

"Oh?" she tipped her head.

"Yep," I slapped my buns and they twanged. "Firm, real firm," I said.

The clerk cleared her throat, nodded and rang up the ticket, "I told you that girdle is one of our best sellers. It will be $14.95."

While writing the check I turned my head to one side and asked, "Have you ever heard of that home video show on T.V.?"

"What?" she looked at me strangely.

"Never mind," I said hoping this meant there had been no hidden camera in the dressing room number three.

As I handed her the check and walked toward the door I prayed I would be able to drive safely in this thing. What if the pressure got too great and this Michelin girdle blew while I was driving? What if I had a wreck? What if I had to tell the policeman that the girdle made me do it? And...I began to sweat.

Dee Dee and I were pretty good friends. Maybe she could be sworn to secrecy and help cut me out of this thing.

Then with a smile I thought, should I have a blow-out on the way home, at least I would know where a very healthy spare was!

Scraps of Laughter
for Ladies

Phone Calls

I am not a telephone talker. Not much anyway. All our kids have jobs and busy lives. Two of them work the night shift. Three of them work twelve-hour shifts, so I let them call me because I don't want to catch them sleeping. Yet, I love those calls. They can make my day…and sometimes break my day.

When my phone rang, I was washing dishes. Always I am glad for an excuse to dry my hands and sit for a while. It was Tandolynn.

"Mom," she whispered.

"Tandolynn is there something wrong?" I asked.

"No."

"Then why are you whispering?"

"Because I don't want Kelloway to hear. She's in the bathroom, so I don't have very much time, but I had to tell you what happened," She muffled a giggle.

"So, tell me. What happened?" I wanted to know.

"Mom, Kelloway started this new diet she found online. The first step is to take Magnesium Citrate."

"Why, and what is that for?" I asked.

Tandolynn giggled again, "It is a laxative, and I'll let you guess what it is for!"

I shook my head and laughed.

"Mom, we had to go to a drugstore to find it. The cute guy at the checkout counter was the only checkout person, and Kelloway begged me to go through with her Magnesium Citrate." She laughed, "I told her, 'no way!' But when he picked up that box to scan, he started reading it out loud, 'Magnesium

141

Scraps of Laughter
for Ladies

Citrate. I haven't sold any of this before.' Then he asked Kelloway what it was for? Kelloway turned red and shrugged her shoulders. So, that guy turned the box over and started reading the back out loud. 'A heaping tablespoon… mix in water… best used at bedtime…' Then this wicked smile tip-toed over his lips as raised his eyebrows and mumbled an 'ooohhh!' He grinned, winked at Kelloway, scanned that box and tossed it in a sack. Kelloway turned beat red and told him it was for her grandma! Mom, we laughed so hard, but Kelloway made me promise not to tell anybody! But I had to tell you!"

I laughed. "LouBelle!" that is Tandolynn's nick name, "I would have given anything to see that!"

"It was great, Mom, but I got to go. I hear her spraying, and that means she'll be out of the bathroom any minute! Love you."

I hung up the phone and thought I really need to make a diary of my phone calls.

Mostly Greg and I live in our fifth wheel, so in the icy winter months we schedule meetings in Texas, Arizona and New Mexico. I don't miss the cold, but I do long for the beauty of the snow or frosted trees with their branches bowing to the drifts of white beneath them. That was where my thoughts had been wondering when the phone rang. It was Kelloway, which cheered my heart.

"Mom, I hate South Dakota!" she growled into the phone.

"Honey, what happened?" I spoke calmly to soothe her.

"The snow, Mom, the snow! It snows all the time! I hate the snow! I went to Walmart to get a scoop shovel, and they were all sold out! So, I had to find a

Scraps of Laughter
for Ladies

neighbor to borrow a scoop from. Finally, the fifth neighbor clear down at the end of the block from me was home and let me use her shovel!"

"Well, Honey, that helps to get to know your neighbors. And it is a good thing to be able to call on your neighbors." I reasoned with her.

"I don't want to know them. I want it to quit snowing and blowing and icing!" Kelloway moaned.

"I'm sorry, Honey. If I could make the weather better for you I would," I said.

"I wish you could!" she grumbled. "My driveway slopes up, and my car couldn't even get up the driveway until I scooped a path for my it. And then," her voice rose, "and then, my car wouldn't go up the drive because there was ice underneath the snow, and it was too slick, and the scoop wouldn't chop the ice! I had to go back to Walmart to get Ice Melt to throw on my driveway just so I could drive up it! AND, right by the door going into Walmart do you know what I saw?" she didn't give me time to answer. "I saw a whole big box of scoop shovels! I grabbed one and told the Walmart worker, 'It's about time you got snow scoops in! I wish they had been here a little while ago. I needed one.'

Mom, that worker winked at me and said, "I watched you come in about an hour or so ago. If I had known you were looking for a scoop, I would have told you they were right here. This is the snow scoop spot, here, by the front door all through the winter months…September through the first of June!" He sounded like he was going to go on forever, so I cut in and asked him, "Snow melt?"

He pointed to it, "Right beside the scoops."

143

Scraps of Laughter
for Ladies

"Mom, he said the winter months are September through the first of June! Do you know how long that is? I hate this place!"

I swallowed, "Kelloway, you will get used to it, and if that is the worst thing that happens, you can do it. Snow melts. Remember, 'I can do all things through Christ which strengtheneth me.'"

"I don't want to remember that, Mom. I don't want to do all things. Especially, I don't want to scoop snow in June!"

"Did the ice Melt work?" I tried to change the subject.

It didn't work.

She butted in, "And, that is not THE WORST! When I got home and spread the ice melt, I opened the garage door and drove my car in to keep it warm for going to work in the morning. Mom, the garage door would not close! It was frozen open! I hate South Dakota!"

Quietly I asked, "Honey, did you get it closed, maybe that neighbor you met down the street?"

"Oh, I got it closed, and I didn't need the neighbor down the street! Which was good because she must be 82! I got a ladder and climbed up high enough to grab ahold of the bottom of the garage door, and I swung on it until I finally got it almost closed! I hope it will open in the morning, so I can get to work! I hate the snow! I hate the ice! I hate South Dakota!" The anger in her voice hit a crescendo.

I smiled. How many of her temper tantrums had I been through with her? "Kelloway, fix you some soup, curl up in a blanket, and watch your favorite comedy. Tomorrow, this will be over, and you might even be able to laugh. Remember, Daddy and I love

144

Scraps of Laughter
for Ladies

you, but God loves you more. Talk to Him. He will take care of you even if you are living in South Dakota! God knows where South Dakota is, He made it."

When we hung up, I cradled my phone to my chest. Man, I love her, and I want her to reach out to the Lord.

The next time the phone rang it was Tandolynn. My heart warmed, "Hi, Honey."

Tandolynn giggled, "Mom, I have to tell you something funny."

"Good," I told her, "I like funny."

"Mom, I had to get my car inspected, and Boone and Clay told me there was no way it would pass inspection. They said my car needed new tires, but, you know, I cannot afford new tires! Not right now! I'm in school. So, I thought about it, until I came up with an idea that I figured just might work. To make this idea better, I bet my brothers that I wouldn't have to get new tires. So, this morning, I dressed very nice. I curled my hair and put my make-up on. Mom, when I drove into the inspection place, about five different guys asked if they could help me. I told them I just needed an inspection. They took my car, offered me a bottle of water or soda or anything I wanted. They were gone a whole of maybe five minutes, revved it up, backed it out of the garage and all five guys handed me that inspection sticker. My car passed!" she laughed. "And best of all, my brothers owe me!"

Now I did not teach her this way of persuasion. She learned it on her own! But we enjoyed the laughter it brought. When our mirth subsided, she told me she needed to talk to dad. I put her on the speaker phone. First, I made her tell her father what she had done. He

145

laughed, too, and made some comments about being just like your mother. It must be a girl thing.

"Dad, I hate mowing the lawn!" she began.

I laughed as her daddy told her, "It was your idea, Tandolynn."

I chuckled as I remembered when we had left for our travels that May. We had told her we would find someone to mow the lawn. She told us if we would get a lawn mower, she would keep it mowed. I remember raising my eyebrows…Tandolynn mowing the lawn? But she assured us she would like mowing, and it would be a good workout for her. So…we got her a lawn mower.

I tapped her daddy on the shoulder, "Honey, remind her that the mower was her idea."

Tandolynn heard me.

"Mom, the next time I have an idea like that just kill me. Put me out of misery! I hate mowing the lawn. And I need a new string for the weed eater, Dad. What kind of string does it take, or what number is it?" she asked.

Dad groaned, "I don't keep those things written in my mind, Girl. Go to the shed. I think there is a spool of the string in there, or at least an empty spool you could get the number from."

Tandolynn whined, "Dad, I can't go in that shed."

"Yes, you can, Tandolynn. The key is by the back door."

"No, Dad. The key is not the problem. I know where the key is. That is not why I can't go into the shed. Dad, there is a big spider that lives in there, and last time I went in the shed that spider ran at me and almost got on me."

Scraps of Laughter
for Ladies

Her daddy laughed, "Tandolynn, you can't not go in the shed because there is a spider in there. That doesn't make any sense. Just kill the spider."

"Dad, I'm not a trophy hunter. That spider is a really big spider, and it's hairy, and it is fast! And, for all I know it might be poisonous!" she reasoned.

Her daddy sighed, "Okay, Tandolynn. Just inside the door of the shed is an insect sprayer. Grab it and spray the spider with it."

Tandolynn wailed, "Dad, I can't. The spider lives right there on that insect sprayer!"

Greg rolled his eyes, so I grabbed the phone and came to the rescue, "Tandolynn, I have an idea. You need new string for the weed eater?"

"Yes," she dragged out the word.

"Then why don't you take the weed eater to Pride Home Center, carry it in and ask what kind of string you need for it. Tell them your dad is an evangelist. He is way out of Amarillo, maybe in Oregon or somewhere and he won't be home for months, so you have no one to even tell you what kind of string it takes. I am sure the guy will help you, and he may even load the string into the weed eater for you. After all you are still dressed for this kind of job, aren't you?"

"I sure am. I haven't changed yet. Great idea, Mom! Thanks, Dad!" She hung up the phone.

Her daddy looked at the silent phone. "I didn't even do anything," He spread his hands wide, but he laughed. "Women!"

I smiled, "I love my phone calls!"

Scraps of Laughter for Ladies

Just Campin'

When I married Greg, I knew he was going to be a pastor. I just didn't know the wide avenue that was opened before me concerning camps. There was Jr. camp, Sr. camp, and Winter camp. I don't even know how many camps I have been to throughout our forty-some years, but many memories are etched in my mind.

My first time being a counselor for Jr. Camp was at Camp Bloom, held in an old school building on the edge of a dying town next to a cemetery in western Kansas. The classrooms were used as dorm rooms stashed with bunk beds. One side of the hall was for girls and the other for boys. The gym was for chapels, and deep down in the dungeon, tucked beneath the gym, were the shower rooms. On my first trip down those chipped cement steps, I gasped, turned around, and tromped back up the stairs. There were three showers. A wooden crate was laid in the bottom of each shower, but there were no shower curtains.

I found Greg, "This is not going to work. There are no shower curtains. There is no way I am going to take a shower with third, fourth, and fifth grade girls watching. I am seven months with child, and I look like I am 13 months along. It would distort their minds."

"Ah, Hon, they won't care," he smiled.

"I will," I told him.

He shrugged, "Then wait 'til we get home."

I narrowed my eyes. "This is Monday. We don't go home until Friday, and this is Kansas in July, 103-degree weather!"

149

Scraps of Laughter
for Ladies

He sighed, "Tell you what, while we are in the chapel, you can go down and shower. I'll watch our girls."

That sounded good. I went to chapel with my towel draped over my shoulders. The moment the preacher got up and started, I grabbed my shower bag and headed to the dungeon. It was still steamy. I scooted the one chair beside the shower I was going to use and placed my towel over the back and my hair stuff on the seat. I turned on the water and stepped in. Oh, it felt good. I closed my eyes and suds up.

Then I heard a deep gasp.

My eyes flew open. Three junior girls were frozen in place, mouths dropped open and staring at me.

I screamed, and so did they just before they turned, tumbling over each other, and shot up the stairs.

I pulled in a deep breath and shoved my head back under the water. That would be three girls who would never wish to have babies.

When I met Greg after chapel, he told me our sound effects had been perfect. The walls of Jericho had just fallen.

While Greg and I were in Texas, we took the teens to Silver State Youth Camp. This group of girls was a rowdy bunch. They came to me in my bunk. They were up before they were supposed to be, so I told them to go back to their bunks. It seemed there was a problem in the bathroom with one of the commodes. I raised my eyebrows. Tandolynn was not quite two, and I didn't want them to wake her up. "Listen, I can't fix a commode, so you will have to find the dorm mom."

Scraps of Laughter
for Ladies

They whined, "But it will be too late. There is going to be yuk water all over the floor."

"Alright." I crawled out of my bunk, and we headed to the bathroom.

"Where?" I asked.

"Right here," They grinned and pushed me into a stall. Then a couple of girls grabbed my arms and yelled, "Swirly time!"

I didn't know what a swirly was, but I wasn't going to have one.

From behind, someone grabbed my head and tried to dunk it in the commode. Now, I am a farm girl, and no one is going to stick my head in a commode and flush it. The fight was on. I whipped about and swung one of the girls around, landing her broadside the toilet bowl with her hand dipped deep into the dark depths of water. That bowl teetered off its seal. Water sprayed from underneath, and the girls let go of me like a hot cake and ran wildly. When I stepped out of that bathroom, the dorm mom was heading their way. I smiled. They were in trouble and got K.P. But I still planned to get even for the injustice they tried to serve me. I went down to the rodeo arena, gathered a bunch of horse apples, and stashed them in each of their pillowcases. They didn't find them until the long, hot ride home to Texas.

Another memory pressed into my mind. It was early June when my sister Cathy and I cooked for our Jr. Camp on the edge of Palo Duro Canyon in Texas. We didn't have to fix lunch on Wednesdays because the first camp had gone home, and the next camp didn't come in until evening. Together, we decided to explore an old, deserted farmhouse. We had to scale the fence and dodge the cows, but we loved the exploring. Old houses have such character and history. However, Cathy refused to go into the dark basement with me. I begged. I just knew that would be where we would find treasures. We had brought a flashlight, but she was stubborn and would not give in, so I gave up exploring the basement. I was not brave enough to do it alone. Besides that black hole was dark and musty, and Texas land is infested with rattlesnakes. But the attic was a different story. Light streamed in the broken windows, yet Cathy wouldn't budge. "Okay," I told her, "You will miss out."

Slowly, I went up the creaky stairs, surprised at how dark it was. There were only two tiny attic windows. I stood at the top of the stairs, taking a deep breath, suppressing an urge to run back down them, but Cathy would laugh and say, "I told you so." Quickly, I crossed the threshold, tripped, and almost fell. A swarm of bats screeched, and like a cloud, they swirled about my head before they flew out the windows.

My breath was gone. I couldn't even scream, and I thought I was going to wet my pants. I dropped my drawers and squatted; after all, no one lived there…well, except the bats.

"Hey, Sandy?" my sister called from below, "Are you alright? Did you spill your water 'cause it's leaking through the ceiling?"

I giggled uncontrollably until my sister edged up the stairs to check on me. She surveyed the situation, put a hand on her hip, and put one in the air to measure a pinch. She said, "You missed me by this much!" She snapped her fingers in the air. "No way would I forgive that." She turned and stomped back down the stairs, but I did hear her snickering.

Scraps of Laughter
for Ladies

Without a doubt, I would say the worst camp experience I have had was at Outdoor Ed. When I taught school, the fifth graders would go on an overnight campout at Hidden Falls Ranch. They needed teachers to be dorm counselors…glorified babysitters. Since I had so much camp experience, I was asked to go. There were eight girls on my side of the cabin. By the time night came, and we had sung and told ghost stories around the campfire, those girls were wound up, and I was tired. Like a mother hen, I gathered them, drew sticks for shower order, four at a time, and settled them around my bed. Then, we had a story and a prayer. After they were tucked in and sleeping soundly, I grabbed my shower bag and tip-toed into the bathroom. I looked at the shower curtains and shook my head. Camp. Who would pick transparent shower curtains with yellow ducks strewn over them? I hung my towel over the curtain rod suctioned to the shower sides and seized my body wash. After the long day we had had, this shower sure felt good.

Now, on the backside of our bathroom is the bathroom of the other bunkhouse. You know how girls are. No one goes to the bathroom alone. All the girls on the other side decided to go to the bathroom. When they flushed, it took every drop of my cold water!

HOT! HOT! HOT!

I jumped backward from the boiling spray and got tangled in the shower curtain. I fought that plastic sheet with the flock of ducks blocking my escape route. The suctioned bar securing the shower curtain banged on my head then crashed to the floor. My shower curtain was still hooked on the bar, pulling me

Scraps of Laughter
for Ladies

down. I tripped, fell and rolled. I was wound like a pig in a blanket.

The bathroom door flew open, and my eight fifth-grade girls rushed in to surround me. Their eyes were wide, and their mouths hung open.

In a panic, I yanked a yellow duck over a couple of my private places.

"Are you okay, Mrs. Waggoner?" Tiffany asked.

I nodded in a lie.

"Do you want us to go find the nurse?" Carmen asked.

"No," I shook my head.

"Do you want us to help you up?" Kayla offered.

"No. I'll manage. I want all of you to go crawl back into your bunks."

Slowly, they filed out, and I heard Tiffany say, "Did you see her face?"

"I did, and I'll never forget it! All that black stuff!" Kayla whistled. "She must have hit her face. Wait 'til I tell Mom!"

"Shhh, she'll hear you," Tiffany warned.

"I heard that," I called.

"I told you," Tiffany whispered.

Then I yelled a warning, "No telling moms! What happens at camp stays at camp!"

The door swished shut. I rolled to unwind from the flock of ducks shower curtain, got to my knees, and crawled to the sink to pull myself off the cement floor. As I stood in front of the mirror, I blinked. Black mascara streaked my cheeks and smudged over my nose. Yes. Those eight fifth-grade girls will remember Mrs. Waggoner. Forever! Somehow, I would have to

Scraps of Laughter
for Ladies

pray that I could impress in their minds, "What happens at camp stays at camp!"

I made another lasting memory at a ladies' retreat a couple of years ago. The strangest thing happened. I was at the top of the A-frame cabin. I had both sides to myself. However, there was no bathroom, so a flashlight became an extra appendage. At night, I would quietly tip-toe to the door, over the porch, down the stairs, and across the campground to the ladies' bath house. This is the time I figured I would see a bear! Yet so far, so good. No bear. Well, once I ran into my husband. He can be pretty growly.

Each morning, I would get up at five a.m. and take my shower. That way, I have plenty of alone time to start my day. The week had been good when Friday rolled around. Friday was clean-up and go-home day. Still, I got up at five for my shower, but I was tired. I looked longingly at my bed when I returned to my bunk. I was cold, my hair was wet, and I wanted to cuddle. I crawled beneath the sheets…for just a couple of minutes. Two hours later, I woke up. I rolled over and nabbed my phone. I touched the screen. "Seven thirty-seven? Seven thirty-seven! Oh, no, seven thirty-seven! We eat at 8:00, and it is seven thirty-seven! It can't be!"

I jumped out of bed. I still had my wet towel wrapped around my head and my nighty on. And boy, oh boy, did I have to go to the bathroom! That meant…out the door…over the porch…clear across camp…and no real clothes on! I was in big trouble. I tried digging through my luggage for clothes but couldn't stand still. I plopped on the bed and crossed my legs, taking deep breaths. My eyes searched the room for help and landed on the trash can. The trash can. Yes. The trash can! There was a trash bag in it and a roll of paper towels on the windowsill. I could wad up some of those paper towels, and they would soak up everything I was holding inside…I hoped.

Now, the trash can was plastic, about 18 inches tall and rectangular, but I was sure it would work. It had to work. I sat it where the wall slanted to meet the floor so I could hold onto a rafter to steady things. I eased down on the trash can. It worked, and I was feeling so much better. Then that plastic waste basket buckled! It buckled and shot out from underneath my buns. With a loud Ker whap, I crashed onto the floor!

There was a moment of quiet, and then, from below, the ladies called, "Is everything okay up there?"

I was afraid they were at the bottom of the stairs, ready to run up. No one could see me like that! "All is great," I answered and prayed they would not come up to check on me. I just dropped some stuff." It was kind of true?

I think camp makes me tell lies!

My husband met me as I came down the stairs, gently holding my trash sack.

"Let me take that for you, Honey." He reached for my bag. His eyebrows furrowed. " It feels like liquid. Did you spill something?"

I smiled, "Sort of."

He watched me take a few steps, then wrapped his arm around me. "Honey, you are walking with a limp. What happened?"

My eyebrows rose, and my smile wrapped nearly around my face, "I will tell you when we drive off this campground, and not until!"

As we turned onto the main road, he ordered, "Out with it, girl. What happened?"

Scraps of Laughter
for Ladies

I poured out my story.

He gulped, "That was the bag of trash I carried, wasn't it?"

I nodded.

And my wonderful husband? He and I laughed all the way down that winding mountain road to Cascade, Idaho!

Scraps of Laughter
for Ladies

The Dentist

I have never liked dentists. As a child, I remember going to the dentist. We always got a squishy, rubbery animal of our choice if we were a good patient, but the event that is etched in my memory forever is my one and only feeling. Vaguely, I remember the shot and the fuzzy, lazy feeling that blanketed me. After holding my mouth open at yawning widths with a glistening stream of drizzle steadily trickling from the corner of my lips, over my chin, and down my neck, my dentist switched the drill off and told me to rinse. I turned my head in the direction of the mini sink and aimed. I didn't understand. My lips and the lower half of my face were numb. Like a geyser, gritty water spewed towards the sink, over me, the floor, and one whole side of my dentist. The only place I felt wet was where it soaked through my shirt to the fleshy part of my arm.

With just a hint of a smile, my dentist said, "Next time, you might want to close your lips while you rinse, and here's a towel for your chin."

I took the towel and blubbered something like, "blanbx u-blub."

Over the years, my love for dentists never changed. I avoided them at all costs, or sometimes because of the cost, until I had pain. Even then, I waited until it turned into root canal pain.

Now, the dentist I found was a very good one, but as he had me eyeball the x-ray of my tooth root, I broke out into a cold sweat. I am not even sure what he explained to me, and it was a good thing his secretary gave me a card with the date, or I would have forgotten that, too.

As the day drew near, I prayed I would get sick. No such luck fell my way. That summer day dawned bright and sunny. I did everything right. I read my Bible and prayed. I even ate breakfast to calm my heart. I brushed and flossed my teeth three times, and when nothing else could be done except get in the car and be on my way, I did. I prayed all the way there.

The secretary smiled at me when I inched through the door. The nurse was sweet as she told me to follow her, but my mind flashed to the Nazis and the Jews. Follow me? Right! Right, to where?

When we got to the room, she took my glasses, and I felt better that the dentist would only be a blur. As she settled me in the chair, she asked, "Would you like gas?"

I blinked. "Gas?" I asked, remembering the Jews and Nazis again. I lifted my hands from the arms of the chair.

She smiled and nodded.

"Why?" I wanted to know.

Again, she smiled. "Gas relaxes people."

I needed to relax, alright, but somehow, gas and Jews still rang a bell. "Just how is this 'gas' given?" I wanted to know.

She reached up and pulled this mask from somewhere behind me, holding it in front of my face while she explained, "This mask attaches over your nose and around your head."

By then, I was pressed against the chair so much that I'm sure my head had made an indention.

She continued. "The gas really is a relaxing agent. You won't hardly feel the needle, and some of our patients even fall asleep. It will be all over before you know it."

I swallowed. "Boy, that is tempting." And it was. Imagine not feeling a thing and it being over before I knew it. What if I did go to sleep? Wow, oh wow!"

The nurse gently patted my arm and said, "I promise: if you don't like it, you just let us know, and we will turn it off."

I only hesitated a bit. "Sold," I said.

I know a tinge of panic flushed over me when that mask snapped into place, but not for long. I remember the blurry dentist wedging my mouth open a mile wide with something like a semi-jack and the nurse sticking a mini-irrigation pipe into my mouth to suck up the drool delicately. I wondered how I would let them know if this gas was not working. Then, from a distance, I heard the drill begin, which, with time, changed into Heaven's harps and angels singing. I was amazed. I only felt a couple of small needle pokes, and my whole body went mildly numb.

I was relaxed, but somewhere along the line I began quoting every verse of scripture I had ever learned. I was floating, and I was pretty sure soon I would see the gates of Heaven and be in the presence of Jesus.

EARTHQUAKE!

Suddenly, my body erupted, and I began a crash landing back to earth. The nurse yanked that gas mask off my face, and about four people were attacking me with towels and wiping me down. From somewhere far away, the dentist calmly spoke, "Sandy…Sandy? Sandy?"

"UHHH…guug?" I grunted.

161

Scraps of Laughter
for Ladies

Someone pulled the semi jack out of my mouth, but it didn't help my speech any.

"Sandy?" the dentist tried again. "Sandy, you've had a little accident."

Little accident? I didn't understand.

The nurse was dabbing my face and my neck.

"Huuugh?" I mumbled.

"You've vomited a bit."

I tried to say, "I did?" But I think it was more like, "Yug dud?"

Kindly, the nurse asked me if I would like to go to the bathroom and clean up a little.

Things still hadn't registered with me, but I nodded. If they thought I needed to clean up, I guess I needed to clean up. I rolled out of the chair and struggled to stand. The nurse grabbed my arm to help me. Another nurse handed me the top of a pair of scrubs and suggested I might want to change my shirt while I was in the bathroom. They walked me to the bathroom door, slipped me in, and closed it behind me.

When the door shut, I slowly looked at the walls, the ceiling, and the floor. Finally, I remembered and peeled off my blouse. I put on the scrub top. It was snug, but I got it snapped. I fumbled with the doorknob, giggled, twisted it open, and sauntered back to my room. Sweetly, the nurse asked me how I was, and I guess I told her I was okay.

A dental hygienist in training helped me back in my chair. As she raised it, I felt like I could reach out and touch the ceiling. When the nurse turned around, she gasped, "Drop that chair, Deedee! Drop that chair! Don't put her that high!"

My chair torpedoed down, and I giggled hysterically.

Scraps of Laughter
for Ladies

When the dentist stepped back into my room, he asked, "Sandy, do you want to finish this today, or would you like to reschedule?"

Violently, I shook my head. By now, I knew there was no way I would ever come again, and my mouth was already numb.

The dentist smiled and picked up his drill. "I guess we will pass on the gas this time," he chuckled at some unknown joke.

I heard the others in the room snickering.

The rest of the procedure went well, I guess, because they finally roused me out of my chair and, with a smile, walked me to the counter to pay.

The secretary looked up, raised her eyebrows, and swallowed a gasp. Quickly, she told me the amount, and I think I wrote the check. "I'll hold this for you until later," she half smiled.

The nurse had not left my side. When I looked at her, she asked, "Are you going straight home, Sweetie?"

I blinked and shrugged my shoulders. I know I had planned on getting groceries, but I really didn't feel like it now. Still, I asked, "Why?"

The nurse smiled. "Well, you might want to clean up before you leave."

I nodded, and she led me to the bathroom again. I stepped in and closed the door. My wadded-up shirt was on the floor. I looked around for something to put it in and finally found a small bag under the sink. As I was stuffing the shirt into the bag, I looked into the mirror and gasped. Thick streaks of black eye makeup stretched from my eyes to my chin. Some puke chunks were stuck to my cheeks and matted in my hair. The snaps on the scrubs were whipper-jigged and bulging open in places. One snap wasn't. It gaped wide, revealing a hunk of belly skin.

My shoulders sagged as I turned on the water. Scrub as I might, that eye makeup was so waterproof I could have made a commercial! I ended up with smeared gray cheeks and wet clumps of hair. At least I could snap the scrubs right, and if I sucked in my gut, they didn't bulge…too much.

There was a light tapping on the door, followed by, "Sandy, are you all right?"

"Yes." I lied. I would never be all right again. I took a deep breath and opened the door. I smiled at the nurse, who was watching me with her hand over her mouth. I straightened my shoulders and walked past the secretary's raised eyebrows and through the waiting room. Every eyeball followed me. As I pushed the outside door open, I heard a quivering voice say, "Mommie, did you see that? It ain't Halloween, and I ain't going back there!"

Honey, I thought, I ain't going back there again either! As the door swished closed, I smiled, or rather, my numb face did something. The man coming my way dropped his mouth open and stepped clear off the sidewalk to let me pass. I reached my car, stuck the key in the lock, opened the door, and slid in. As I sat, three snaps on the scrubs popped open. I hung my drooping cheeks on the steering wheel and moaned. It was going to be a long ride home!

Scraps of Laughter
for Ladies

The Tip

A few years ago, my husband went to a gathering of ministers. I'm not sure what the main theme of the meeting was, but he came home with a goal. One thing shared at the meeting was a survey of waitresses. The consensus of the survey showed that ministers were the worst clientele ever waited on. Very seldom did the ministers leave tips, and if they did tip, the tips were puny. They also were scored to have a very bad temperament.

After the meeting, my husband and a group of ministers met at a restaurant. As the waitress began taking orders, my husband asked, "Who would you say are your most difficult customers?"

She paused, bit the end of her pencil, and thought. When she had her answer ready, she pointed her pencil at him and said, "Ministers."

A silence followed.

Suddenly, a look of horror crossed her face, and she gasped, "You're not a minister, are you?"

My husband laughed, "You got it, Ma'am, and so is the rest of this sorry bunch!"

Her shoulders dropped as she scanned the table. "I'm sorry," she said, took the orders, and left.

Everyone had a good laugh, but from then on, my husband was determined to change the waitress world's opinion of ministers.

Now, he leaves a substantial tip when we go to any restaurant. In fact, there have even been times when I have wanted to grab the tip, rush to the check-out counter, and make change for it! When he leaves a

Scraps of Laughter
for Ladies

tip at McDonald's, I turn a blind eye and motion for one of the kids to pick it up and shove it into their pocket. After all, he makes the children clean everything off the table, so there is nothing for a worker to do.

Not only did his goal become to leave healthy tips, but also to leave happy waitresses. He is determined to cheer them up. He jokes with them and teases them. Quite often he leaves 'for fun' tips as well as money. They are tips like, 'Don't stand out in the rain,' 'Don't eat bananas without peeling them first,' and 'Be sure your shoes match in public.'" But his favorite tip has to be, 'Don't take any wooden nickels.' Then, when the waitress is happy, he slips her one of our church tracts and invites her to our services. All the waitresses know him, remember him, and welcome him back with a smile.

We have been living this way for several years, and it does work well. I've watched it time after time, and I have yet to see his method fail.

A while back, my husband took me for a coke 'dip date' at the Dip store. We have four children, and sometimes, we have an overwhelming need to escape. Usually, we don't have much time or money, so we do a "dip date." That means we leave our kids with our oldest, drive to the Dip store a couple of blocks away, buy a 99-cent Coke, and head home. On this particular date, my husband and his routine were going well. The cashier was smiling and even chuckling. As we paid for our coke and began to say our farewells, I decided to slip one of my husband's 'for fun' tips in, before he could. The one that came to mind was, 'Don't take any wooden nickels.' Widely smiling, I blurted out, "Here's a tip for you: don't take any wooden nipples!"

166

Scraps of Laughter
for Ladies

The cashier blinked, smiled, and promised, "Believe me, I won't."

I gasped as I realized what I had said. I stuttered and backtracked. "I meant wooden NICKLES!" I guess I was trying so hard to leave the tip before my husband did that my tongue tripped on my teeth.

"Nickles," I repeated, "Not…a…nipples."

My husband's eyes bugged out. He grabbed my arm and yanked me out the door. "Why did you say that?" he demanded as if I had said it on purpose.

I blinked. "I didn't mean to say that. Probably she didn't even notice," I rationalized.

"Are you kidding? Didn't you see her mouth drop open?" he asked. "It almost hit the counter!"

I shook my head, "It's okay, Honey." I began to giggle, "Besides that, she doesn't even know us, and it most likely gave her a good laugh for the day. That's your goal, isn't it? Leave them smiling."

"Ha! I left a tract with the church name on it, and my name is on it, too!" He opened the car door for me, walked around to the other side, and slid under the wheel.

By now, I was more than giggling. I was laughing. My husband tried very hard not to laugh, but by the time we reached home we were both about to die.

For weeks he refused to take me for a dip date.

In the days that followed, anytime we checked out of one place or another I would gently nudge him in the side and ask, "You want me to leave a tip?" A knowing look would pass between us, and we would begin to laugh.

Finally, the Dip date tip died down and things settled back to normal until one Sunday morning. We

167

Scraps of Laughter
for Ladies

sang songs and listened to the announcements when I noticed a visitor across the aisle from me. I smiled at her and began to think she looked familiar, but I couldn't place her. Every now and then I'd slip a glance in her direction to see if I could remember where we'd met. Nothing clicked. Then my husband began introducing our guests. "Mrs. Nancy Nickles," he said, and she stood.

I slammed my head toward her, looked at her, and drew a sharp breath. "NICKLES!" I gasped to myself, "The Dip Store!" Quickly I dropped my head. Surely her name couldn't be Nickles! NO! I felt laughter welling up inside of me. I had to do something, or I was going to explode. Quietly, I stood and walked down the aisle, out the door, and practically ran into the bathroom. Tremors shook my body. I began to laugh uncontrollably. I leaned against the wall and sank to the floor, very unladylike. Tears began rolling down my cheeks.

I didn't see the two little girls standing before me until I wiped my eyes.

"Are you okay, Mrs. Pastor?" the wide-eyed girls asked.

I swallowed and nodded while still laughing. The two girls backed away from me and piled out the door.

I had to control myself. I bit my lip and took deep breaths. Finally, the laughter eased. Then I heard a light tapping on the door. I swallowed. "Yes?" I asked.

The usher's deep voice sounded, "Do you need some help there, Ma'am? These girls said something was wrong with a lady sprawling out on the floor."

"Oh! Yes, I mean, No! Everything's fine now.

Scraps of Laughter for Ladies

I've got it under control!" I assured him.

"Okay, Ma'am, but I'll get someone if you need me too!"

"No! No need, but thanks!"

He paused for a minute before I heard him step away from the door.

I held my breath, pulled myself off the floor, and went to the sink. With cold water, I washed my puffy face. I dug in my purse for some make-up and smothered it on. It didn't look good, but it would have to do. I took a deep breath and stepped out the door. The usher looked at me with a question in his eye.

I nodded that all was well.

Church was almost over, so I slipped into the back pew and sat down. The two little girls from the bathroom were beside me. They looked at me, then at each other, and scooted to the other end of the pew.

When the final amen was said, I joined my husband at the back door to shake hands. One of the last to leave was Nancy Nickles. I prayed, "Please, Lord, help me not laugh!" She shook my hand, and I smiled widely while biting my cheek. I was so thankful. I had made it through just fine. I didn't think she even recognized us. Nancy Nickles pushed the outside door open. My husband waved and said, "Thank you for visiting our services, Mrs. Nipples."

A horrible hush settled.

Slowly, she turned, smiled, and said with a wink. "Pastor, don't take any wooden nickels! And I'll see you next Sunday!" The door eased closed behind her. I jabbed my husband in the ribs, "What did you say that for?"

He started to protest and looked at me, We both laughed uncontrollably.

Scraps of Laughter
for Ladies

"Want to go for a dip date?" he winked. We ran for the car.

Scraps of Laughter
for Ladies

They Stole My Underwear!

It was the last day of November, a cool sweater day with the promise of snow. I had on a jean skirt and a black sweater with a jacket in the truck should I need it. We were on our way to Gallup, New Mexico, for their annual area-wide ladies' meeting. I was excited because I was going to get to speak, and I liked that. I had my lesson, and everything I needed for it was packed, on a list, and checked off twice. I was ready.

In Albuquerque, we decided to stop and eat lunch at Cracker Barrel. We had a gift card, and Greg and I were having a great day. Lunch at Cracker Barrel would top it off. I love the gift shop, and Greg likes the food. Meatloaf is always his favorite, and I think Cracker Barrel must have confiscated his mother's recipe.

After we ate, we pushed back and smiled at each other. Now, my job would be to keep him awake. Greg always gets that snoozy feeling for about thirty minutes after lunch. Usually, all I had to do to wake him was volunteer to drive, and today, we still had to drive through Albuquerque. The streets of that city are wildly alive and… well…hazardous! Just the thought of me driving those streets would keep him awake for hours to come.

I toted my left-over bag as we headed for the pick-up, and Greg pressed the button on his key fob to unlock the doors. We noticed a couple of guys jump into their black car on the other side of our pick-up, back out, put on the gas, and swerve toward the exit of the parking lot.

Scraps of Laughter
for Ladies

"Looks like someone else had a good lunch, too," I smiled.

As I climbed into my seat, I noticed my cell phone was on the console between Greg and me. "That's funny. I don't remember leaving my phone there. If I don't have it with me, I always keep it in my phone holder."

Greg gave me his speech again about taking better care of my phone. I ignored him and switched on our Louis Lamour story again.

A couple of hours later, we pulled into Grace Navajo Mission. Evening shadows were beginning to fall. The crew was still setting up for the ladies' meeting, so Greg and I pitched in to help. We didn't even bother to unload our things. That could wait. We laughed and finished the banquet room. Bro. Ted and Tonie invited us to share a family birthday celebration with them, and as that was where we were staying, we gladly agreed, but first, we asked if we could unload our things before it got dark and cold.

Tonie gave me the key to their house, which was just across the way. I went to open the door while Greg started unloading the pick-up.

Through the clear, crisp air, he called, "Honey, we must have forgotten to load your suitcase."

"What?" In panic, I turned from the door, "No. It has got to be there."

He looked at me through the open pick-up door window, "No. I would have put it right here. That is where I always set your bag."

I walked back down the steps, and with hope I said, "Maybe this time you put my bag in a different place?"

Scraps of Laughter
for Ladies

He shoved his head and shoulders back into the truck and dug. "No. I didn't, Honey, your bag is not here."

I blinked and absently dropped my gaze to the passenger door. "Greg, look. That little keyhole thing is gone from my door. Do you think it fell off while we were traveling?"

Greg gasped and yanked the upper half of his body out of the back seat. "My bag is gone, too. We didn't forget both our bags. We have been carjacked!"

"Carjacked?" I wailed.

"Carjacked," he nodded.

"What can we do?"

"Not much now. I can call the Albuquerque police because Cracker Barrel is the only place we stopped. It had to be jacked there, but that was hours ago. I doubt they can do anything." Greg shook his head. "I guess we had better unload the rest of the things."

God was so good. The jackers had NOT gotten his guitar or our hang-up clothes. Yes! I guess the hang-ups had hidden the guitar! And…they had missed my handbag. But my bible bag was gone, and I found myself hoping they stole themselves a load of 'Jesus' grief. Maybe they would get saved!

We got the rest of the things unloaded and drove to meet Bro. Ted and Tonie at the restaurant. On the way into town we called Tonie to explain. They had reserved a long table for the whole extended family. We were introduced and welcomed just like old friends.

It was hard for me to study the menu because I kept thinking about our losses. Greg got the

Scraps of Laughter
for Ladies

Albuquerque police on the phone, excused himself, and asked me to order for him. I scanned the menu.

The waitress came, and I can't remember what I ordered for Greg or me. Then it hit me, and I gasped, "They took my underwear!"

All my new friends stopped talking, dipping chips, and stared at me.

I turned red and swallowed, "Not the underwear I have on now."

Everyone still looked at me while trying to smile.

Tonie came to my rescue, "The Waggoners had their pick-up broken into in Albuquerque while they had lunch at Cracker Barrel today."

"Cracker Barrel? On the north side of the city?" someone asked.

I nodded my head, "I believe that was the one."

"That is the worst part of Albuquerque, and Cracker Barrel is always getting hit," someone said.

"Do they ever find who did it?" I asked.

Another table member said, "I don't know if they really even try."

I swallowed. Horror filled my eyes as I could see all my underwear decorating the alleys around the Cracker Barrel area. I muttered, "I am sure glad I didn't have my name stitched in my drawers."

"What?" Tonie asked.

I laughed, "I was just kidding, but Mom used to take a permanent marker and write our names in all our under things when I was a girl so my sister and I wouldn't get them mixed up."

Tonie's daughter reached across the table and patted her mother's hand, "Thank you, Mom, for not doing that."

Scraps of Laughter
for Ladies

"I didn't have to, Silly. You were our only girl,"she laughed.

In turn, Tonie's granddaughter gasped and warned her mother, "Don't even think of it, Mother."

Her mother laughed, "There is no place to write on those things you wear!"

"Mother!" her daughter blushed.

We all laughed.

When our food came, Greg and I gobbled it down… quickly…whatever it was…and excused ourselves. We had to go to the stores, and we didn't have very much time before they closed. Oh, Walmart would be open all night, but I needed things I wasn't sure they would have, like a white bra for the lacy, white blouse I had brought to wear while speaking. Those thieves had left me with only the black one I had on, and I just couldn't stand in front of all those ladies with a black bra under a white blouse. Oh, I know the younger generation does that sort of thing, but I didn't feel like following the trend at this time in my life.

And there was no way I could borrow from my friend, Tonie. She is just too skinny! So, Jock Penny's, here I come!

Greg sped to the mall, and we made it thirty minutes before they closed. They had a white bra! Yes! But they did not have a slip. I always wear a slip…even if my skirt has material that is thick enough that no one could possibly see through it... but… because of a childhood memory. When I grew up, there was a lady, who shall remain nameless, in our church who never wore a slip. At the end of the church services, when we would rise to sing the final hymn, she would stand… and… clutched right there in her bun cheeks was her skirt. My sister and I called it a vertical smile, but only when our mom was out of earshot. Forever, that memory will be a pressed (SMILE) in my mind, but hopefully never pressed in my behind! I never wanted that to happen to me. I had to have a slip!

I explained my situation to the lady at the counter. Her eyes rounded with compassion, but she shook her head, "No, we have no slips, Dearie. We haven't carried them for several years. The younger generation does without them." She blinked, rang up the total, and said, "That will be $46.95."

I swiped my J.C. Penny's card and headed for the door. I had to hurry to get to the next store before they closed.

I raced out of Jock Penny's, jumped into the pick-up, and Greg drove me to Cato's. They have nice clothing for a good price, especially if you can get it on sale. I bee-lined to the sales rack. I found a wild and slick, Hippy-looking pair of giant flowered pajama pants. You know. They are the kind of pants people wear to drop their kids off at school or wear to Wally World. They were way too long for me, but for three bucks, I could make them work. I could just roll the elastic of the top up and over several times. Then I grabbed a big but ugly pea-green T-shirt with flowing split sleeves for five bucks. I was only going to sleep in it, and I would probably never wear it again because it was…well, not me! Yet, I needed something to sleep in because we were staying at the pastor's house, and the bathroom was across the hall. It would work, but the slip? I had no luck finding a slip in Cato's either.

Scraps of Laughter
for Ladies

I drudged out of Cato's in disappointment. The only store left that was open now was Walmart, and I didn't think they carried slips.

Walmart was packed even at this time of day. It was the last day of November. I think people had gotten their checks, and those checks were burning holes in their pockets. Greg and I grabbed a cart, pushing our way through the mob to hit the underwear section. Again, I fumed as I thought about my stolen underwear. I just knew they were displayed around some dumpsters in the Cracker Barrel alley. Who knows? Police photo shots might be taken to identify the stolen goods! My checks turned red. How dare they take my underwear! They had been my best drawers because that is what I travel with, and now I was trying to replace them with as cheap of things as I could find. Plus, we needed things like toothpaste, deodorant, shampoo and all that stuff. It was overwhelming.

Finally, Greg and I, with a loaded cart, trudged to the checkout registrar. This was money spent we hadn't planned on, and my husband grudgingly pulled out the bills we had tucked away for the trip home. As he handed them over, he smiled. Along with the money, he slipped a tract of how to get to heaven from Texas in the cashier's hand. "I guarantee that it is possible, Ma'am." He tipped his hat, grabbed the bags, and we walked to the truck.

As I swung the bag of my new underwear, I laughed, "I gave more than a tract today. I gave my bible and all my drawers! Maybe someone will get saved!"

The next day, the ladies' meeting was delightful. However, every time I stood, I carefully and discretely

Scraps of Laughter
for Ladies

pulled my red skirt away from my behind. After the ladies' meeting, my friend Tonie excused me from the gathering before everyone else…and my friend told the tale of my stolen underwear. All these gracious ladies gave and gifted Greg and me with a special love blessing…and it covered everything and more. Isn't God the greatest?!!!

Scraps of Laughter for Ladies

The Bus Stop

Sooo…we had been carjacked in the middle of the day while lunching at Cracker Barrel in Albuquerque, New Mexico. That was Friday. That was just yesterday. We didn't know it at the time, but we found out Albuquerque, New Mexico, is one of America's top cities for crime, and that is trivia I will store away for future use. I now know the traffic is bad, the trafficking is bad, the murder is pretty well up there, and the thieving is sky high. Thus, we will not be stopping in Albuquerque, New Mexico, to sightsee or lunch again. No. We will just zip on through waving and saying, "Been there. Done that."

Anyway, that was my plan.

Saturday morning, my husband wrapped his arms around me and whispered into my hair. "Honey, I know our carjacking is fresh on your mind. I understand it was just yesterday, but tomorrow I must catch the plane to Montana at the Albuquerque airport."

I pulled away from him and narrowed my eyes.

He gently put his forefinger on my lips to hush me before I could say anything else. "Honey, I have been on the phone with Tandolynn. Everything is all worked out. She and Clay have bus tickets to Albuquerque, so as we go through the city, we will pick them up at the bus station, take them with us to the airport, and they will drive you home."

"Clay is coming, too?" I asked.

Greg shrugged, "Tandolynn said she could make her brother do anything she asked. I don't know what hold she has over him, but he's coming with her.

179

Scraps of Laughter
for Ladies

Besides, he didn't like the idea of her riding the bus alone. He's been on a bus before."

I laughed as I remembered his first and last bus trip, "I understand that. I was surprised that Clay hadn't talked his sister out of the bus trip, but the bus was affordable and faster than walking. Those busses are scary, but then Tandolynn has never ridden one before…so she didn't know that yet."

Greg nodded, "I will feel better that she isn't alone on that bus. And it is perfect. Tandolynn is packing a suitcase full of stuff to replace all my stolen things. And," he held his finger in the air, "I had her put in a pair of boots. I would rather not preach in these slip-on work shoes. After all, the whole reason for this Montana meeting is so Bro. Kim Earhart can introduce me to new preachers."

I sighed, "Okay, as long as you promise I don't have to be alone in Albuquerque."

"Promise." He kissed me.

Boots and Jeans opened at 9:00, and we needed to be there as soon as they unlocked the door. At Walmart, we had replaced underwear, sweats, socks, and toiletries, but they did not carry his jeans and western shirts. Hopefully, Boots and Jeans did. We had to hurry because he was singing to open the area-wide ladies' meeting with thirty minutes of the prettiest Christmas tunes you have ever heard. All those ladies think I am the luckiest woman in the world…I just smile. They don't live with him! Really... I wouldn't trade him for anything. Anyway, the ladies' meeting was to start at 11:00. So… we did need to hurry.

Yes! Boots and Jeans had what we needed, and we thanked the Lord because the two shirts we got

Scraps of Laughter
for Ladies

were on sale! We paid at the counter and rushed to our pick-up truck.

We made it back to Bro. Ted and Tonie's home, changed clothes, and headed across the way just in time for the Ladies' Christmas Bash. And just like I said, my hubby sang beautifully, and the ladies loved him. However, he did stand, so his feet were hidden behind a group of red and white poinsettia plants so no one could see his worn shoes. However, I don't suppose any of the ladies looked at his feet.

Sunday morning, Greg told me to be packed early because he wanted to load all our things before church. We had to be ready. He would be doing a concert during the Sunday school hour and then preaching during the morning service. He warned me that our time was short. We couldn't even stay and eat lunch with Bro. Ted and Tonie. We had to get to the Albuquerque bus station, pick up Tandolynn and Clay, and then drop Greg off at the airport. The drive from Gallup was at least two hours long. It was a tight schedule for us. Tandolynn and Clay would have to wait at the bus station for two or three hours, but if **ALL WENT WELL**, we could do it.

I opened the door for Greg to load our things. Great, huge flakes of snow were falling. The ground was already carpeted. Greg shook his head, "Why today? We need every second of time, and it sure would help if the roads were clear."

I shrugged, "It is beautiful, and maybe it is just snowing over Gallup?"

"Right." My husband was grumpy.

Sunday school went well, but just before Greg stepped into the pulpit to preach, his silent phone buzzed. He looked. It was Tandolynn. He handed his

181

phone to me and whispered, "Hun, go out in the lobby and take this call. Make sure everything is alright with Tandolynn."

I slipped out back as he was introduced and stepped to the pulpit.

In the lobby, I answered quietly, "Tandolynn?"

"Mom." I could tell there was a bit of panic in her voice.

"Yes, Honey?" I soothed.

"Mom, our bus driver hasn't shown up yet. We were supposed to leave two hours ago, and the bus driver is not here. They are trying to get another driver, but what are we going to do?"

I took a deep breath. "Are your tickets refundable? I can drive home alone. I am not an invalid."

"No, Mom, they are not refundable."

"But it is their fault, not yours. Surely, they would give you your money back," I reasoned.

"They don't care if it is their fault, Mom. The tickets are not refundable. And you don't need to be driving alone, especially at night."

"But," I started to protest.

She interrupted me. "Mom, they just announced we are boarding, so they must have gotten a driver. I got to go."

"Good. What time should you be in Albuquerque now?"

I could hear her counting the hours, and I had to stop my racing heart when she told me. It would be close. Very close. I put a chipper ring in my voice, "Good, Honey. Good. That means you won't have to wait very long for Dad and me to pick you up at the bus station. We'll all be together before we know it."

Scraps of Laughter
for Ladies

If I had figured it right, there would be no time to spare. Greg and I would pick them up at the bus station, zip over to the airport and Greg would be running to catch his flight.

I inhaled and stepped back into the auditorium. Greg caught my eye with a question. I smiled and gave him an 'all-is-well' nod. I would tell him after services that not all was as well as we had planned. He didn't need to worry about the bus thing while preaching.

When the last amen was said, and all hands shook, Greg sailed out to get the pick-up. I packed the table of CDs and books and waited…and waited. Greg didn't come. When he did, his eyes were sparking. "Honey, we had better pray. The pick-up won't start."

We prayed.

Greg stepped out into about six inches of snow now and made a path to the truck.

I kept praying.

Tandolynn called. "Mom, these stupid morons on the bus started fighting over whose seat is whose and whose isn't whose. The bus driver tried to call them down, but they wouldn't quit yelling long enough to listen. Finally, the driver lurched to a stop, throwing them all over the place. One woman swung her bag and walloped the man alongside his head. He grabbed her by the shoulders to keep from falling, but it caused her to tumble over his whole body. That woman came flying over our seats. She just missed me and almost landed on Clay's head! But she did slide into Clay's lap and sat wobbly before she slid to the floor. Then she turned around and glared at Clay. I think she thought he pushed her, but he promised he didn't. Anyway, the driver pulled over and called 911. And, Mom! I am afraid the driver thinks we were part of the

183

fight! We might end up getting thrown off the bus, and it is cold and snowing outside!" She growled, "I am never riding a bus again!"

"Take a deep breath, Tandolynn, and calm down," I spoke into the phone. "Where are you now?"

"Now? Now?? I don't know…just… we are waiting somewhere out in the middle of nowhere on the highway for the highway patrol to come. The driver doesn't know how long it will take the police to get here, but he refuses to drive a mile more with these messed up morons! Mom! I am never riding on a bus again!"

"Okay. Good. But for right now, just stay close to Clay and call when you are on the road again. I will pray for you, Honey."

"One prayer? You had better send up a bunch of them. That woman just spit on that man! I am never stepping foot on a bus again! I will hitch-hike first."

I quickly said, "Dear Jesus, please be with Tandolynn and Clay," and hung up the phone.

By some miracle of God, our truck started!

Greg drove it over, we loaded our things, gave goodbye hugs, and we were on our way.

As soon as we hit the interstate, Greg began instructing me. "I don't know why the pick-up wouldn't start, Hon, but I think it could be a dead spot in the starter. That means we cannot turn the engine off."

"What? Why?" I asked.

"Because it might not start again, and I don't have time to fix it. Besides, it is Sunday. We might not even be able to get a starter, and I have to catch that plane for Montana."

I nodded. "So… what is the plan?"

Scraps of Laughter for Ladies

"When we hit Albuquerque, we will go straight to the gas station and fill up with fuel. After that, we will go to the bus station and pick up Tandolynn and Clay, then to the airport."

I licked my lips, "About that…There is a good chance their bus won't make it in before your plane flies out."

"What?" he swerved on the snowy road as he swung his head to look at me.

"Tandolynn called just before we left, and it seems there was some kind of altercation on the bus, so the driver pulled off the road and called 911. It sounded like that will take a while. They were still waiting for the highway patrol to come."

If he could have dropped his head in his hands, he would have. Instead, his knuckles turned white while clutching the stirring wheel.

Calmly, he said, "That means no bag. No clothes. No boots to preach in."

I shook my head, "Sorry, Honey."

Greg straightened his shoulders. "Right. We will still fuel up, then we might as well head to the airport."

"Wait," I looked at him, "You can't do that. You have to show me where the bus station is. This is Albuquerque we are talking about. It's a big city. It's the Albuquerque where thugs stole my underwear! You cannot just expect me to drive around and find the bus station on my own." Another thought hit me, "Oh, No! It's a bus station. That means it is probably in the worst part of downtown Albuquerque."

Greg nodded, "Seems likely."

When we pulled into the gas station in that wonderful city, he did not turn off the engine. You can leave it running to put diesel in the tank. I ran to the bathroom. Who knew when I would get a chance again? Then I called Tandolynn, "Honey? Are you on the road yet?"

"Just, but there is no way we will get to Albuquerque before Dad's plane leaves. Those morons are still on the bus."

"I thought the police were coming to take them off."

"It seems the police didn't want them either. Clay and I tried to move further away from them, but no one wanted to be closer to them." She paused, "Mom, I hate buses. I am never going to ride one again."

"You don't have to, Dear," I consoled.

"Mom, have you ever been on one? A bus, I mean?"

"Yes."

"Why didn't you tell me what buses are like?" she accused.

I didn't mean to, but I giggled. "It's an experience you will never forget."

"Believe me, I won't forget it. Oh, no. Mom, I have got to go. That woman is up and waving her bag again."

Before she could hang up, I heard someone yell a few not-so-nice words. Probably the bus driver.

Quickly, I asked, "How long?"

"The driver told us we would get to Albuquerque between 8:00 and 9:00 this evening. Mom, do you realize I could have driven from Amarillo to Albuquerque and back home in less time than that?"

186

Scraps of Laughter
for Ladies

I sighed. It meant I would have to sit and wait at the bus station for four or five hours with the truck running…and most of that time would be after the sun set.

Greg put the bus station on his GPS. And I was right. The station was right in the middle of the downtown 'hood' area of Albuquerque. Slowly, we drove through the streets. Hoodies decorated most of the moving bodies who were wandering about in the cold, snowy alleys and gutters. Some cuddled together while others sprawled about. One dark, tall, hooded fellow stood shaking his fist while chewing out a light post. At least the bus station was not far from the airport. In my mind, I marked the way so I would be able to find my streets back.

We were just in time at the airport to drop off Greg and his borrowed bag; thank you to our friend Bro. Ted and Tonie. He barely even kissed me goodbye. I guess he didn't want to fog my memory of how to get back to the bus station, plus the sun was going down quickly.

I didn't shed a single tear. I guess tears don't come when body-shaking terror takes over.

I did find my way back to the bus station. The tall guy in the dark hoodie had now commenced pounding his head on the light pole. I wanted to park way away from him…but that would be farther from the station. I was in a dilemma. I locked the door…but the passenger door where my carjackers had popped the keyhole out would not lock. I decided I would lean against the driver's door and watch the unlockable passenger's door. That way, no one could sneak up on me.

Scraps of Laughter
for Ladies

I had a bottle of water, which I would only sip because there was no way I could leave the truck running and unlocked to find a bathroom. A few snacks were scattered about the truck, but I wasn't hungry. Besides, snacks would make me thirsty. I had a book I could read, but I couldn't concentrate. I felt an urge to cradle my Bible, yet I couldn't because my Bible had been stolen. Instead, I clutched my cell phone. I could click on my Bible program there.

As the minutes ticked away, I watched the gages. I still had 596 miles of diesel left. That was enough to make it home.

I read a couple of chapters. 591 miles of diesel left.

The street had calmed down. I guessed that the neighborhood had maybe bedded down somewhere else. I looked at the time on my phone then I looked to the dashboard. 589 miles of diesel left.

After three hours and forty-seven long, dark minutes, Tandolynn called. "Mom. Where are you? We are at the bus station, and I don't see the truck anywhere."

"No!" I blared into the phone. "I am at the bus station…unless Albuquerque had another bus station?"

"Mom, don't panic. I'll look it up on my GPS." She began giving me directions. I went down the street, where it dead-ended. I swerved into a parking lot to turn around. I turned on the first street, went a block, and stopped. I gasped. So, this was where all those hooded people went, only they didn't have their hoodies on anymore. They should have been freezing to death, but there were a bunch of bonfires burning. It was some kind of block party, and I couldn't drive through. I backed up the truck and turned around.

Scraps of Laughter
for Ladies

Somehow, I ended up right where I had started from, and there stood Tandolynn and Clay. I was never so glad to see anyone in my whole life.

I guess the bus drives in and unloads on the back side of the station, so I naturally wouldn't see them, nor would they see me.

Clay walked up to my door and swept a gallant bow, "Ma'am, would you like me to drive?"

I nodded, "I would love you to drive."

My legs were wobbly as I stepped out of the truck. Tandolynn opened the passenger door for me (after all, it wasn't locked), but I refused. "I want the back seat…maybe I'll sleep. And could we please stop at the first place we find for a bathroom and maybe something to eat?"

McDonalds it was. With a hamburger, fries, a Dr. Pepper, and Tandolynn's GPS, we left Albuquerque in the dust…or snow. I think Clay made the four-and-a-half-hour trip home in three and a half hours. I don't know for sure because I slept. Oh…and…Greg's flight to Montana landed before we made it home to Amarillo. Life is not fair!

Scraps of Laughter
for Ladies

Show and Tell

I sank my hands into the hot, sudsy dishwater and closed my eyes to let the warmth spread through me. That is the only part about doing dishes that excites me. Tandolynn was down for her afternoon nap, and if I hurried, I could prop my feet up for a while, too.

The telephone rang. I pulled my hands out of the water, grabbed a dish towel, and headed for the phone. I hoped it didn't wake Tandolynn and ruin my afternoon dreams. "Hello," I answered, wedging the receiver between my chin and shoulder while drying my hands.

From the other end of the line came a hesitant voice, "Mrs. Waggoner?"

"Yes," I affirmed.

"Mrs. Waggoner," the voice built up strength, "this is Mrs. Garnell, Boone's teacher."

"Oh, yes," I bubbled, "Boone's teacher. He sure likes school."

She paused, "That's nice."

All of the sudden, I felt very uncomfortable. "Mrs. Garnell, is there a problem with Boone at school?" I asked.

She cleared her throat, "Well…just a minor one."

Scraps of Laughter
for Ladies

I rolled my eyes as I put my hand to my head. Kindergarten! Kindergarten, and already we have problems! Shakily, I asked, "What?"

"Well," again she paused, "listen, I go on break at two this afternoon. That is in about 30 minutes. Do you think you could meet with me then?"

"Sure, "I swallowed quietly and hung up the phone. Quickly, I finished the dishes, woke Tandolynn from her nap, and headed for school.

All the way down the hall, Tandolynn's shoes clicked on the linoleum-covered cement floor. When we reached the kindergarten classroom, I took a deep breath and knocked on the door. The door swung open, and there stood a squatty, little, red-haired girl with big blue eyes. Her eyes popped a little wider as she stared and announced over her shoulder, "Hey! It's Boone's mom!"

All 23 heads flew up and settled their eyes on me. I began to feel a bit uncomfortable.

Mrs. Garnell came to my rescue. "Class, let's line up for music." She clapped her hands, and the little bodies got in line. She smiled, "Mrs. Waggoner, just have a seat over there at the number center. You can let your little girl color on a piece of that paper. I'll be right back." She stepped out the door and headed down the hall with the 23 children toddling behind her.

I took Tandolynn's hand, and we wound through the tables to the number center and waited.

Scraps of Laughter
for Ladies

When Mrs. Garnell returned, she closed the door and headed straight for us. "Please have a seat, Mrs. Waggoner."

I fished for a chair and sat in it. It was a miniature chair, and my knees slid up to meet my elbows.

Mrs. Garnell swallowed, then began. "Mrs. Waggoner, first let me tell you that your little Boone is very bright and creative. In all my 27 years of teaching, I have not encountered a child quite like little Boone."

She paused.

I didn't know whether to say thank you or not because I could just feel there was a bomb about to explode. I was afraid if I said anything, it would push the detonator, so I just sat and looked at her. Tandolynn was oblivious and kept coloring.

Finally, Mrs. Garnell looked up from the papers she had been rustling and said, "Mrs. Waggoner, let me just get to the point. I don't beat around the bush very well. Today in Show and Tell, your little Boone shared that you lounge around at home with no upper garments on."

"What?" I gasped.

"Boone said that you sit around the house half-naked." She looked at me, and I could feel my cheeks burning.

"I do not!" I blurted out and couldn't wait to get my hands on 'little' Boone.

Scraps of Laughter
for Ladies

Tandolynn stopped coloring and looked at me. I could tell she wanted to make me feel better. She shoved her picture toward me and smiled, "Mommy, this is a picture of you."

Both Mrs. Garnell and I dropped our eyes to the picture.

To my horror, it was a stick figure with only a skirt hanging from it. I wailed, "Put a shirt on it!" Then I calmed myself to let my gaze settle on Mrs. Garnell. "I assure you, I am always fully clothed at home."

"Yes, well..." She drummed her fingers on the table and studied me over the top of her glasses, "Frankly, Mrs. Waggoner, I believe you. That is not the problem. You must realize there are 22 other students in my class who will go home and report this to their mamas and daddies."

My eyes grew wide. "They can't do that! My husband is a preacher, and this is a small town!"

"Mrs. Waggoner," she spread her hands wide, "there is not a thing I can do about it now."

"Oh, no!" I was horrified.

"Listen, Mrs. Waggoner," she spoke, "what I would like to suggest is that when we have Show and Tell, and that is every Friday, just be sure that you have little Boone bring something to show. That way, he won't feel he has to tell us something."

"That sounds good to me," I was still shaking.

"Great." She stood and stretched out her hand to me. She walked to the door and stepped out. I grabbed

Scraps of Laughter
for Ladies

Tandolynn's hand and her artwork; then we followed Mrs. Garnell.

The class was coming like a little herd of ants stretching down the hall. As each child passed, they gazed wide-eyed at me. Again, I could feel the blush spread over my face. 'Little' Boone gleamed. Like a bolt of lightning, I snatched him out of that line and smiled at his teacher. "I'd like to have a word with 'little' Boone," I explained.

"Surely." She nodded and closed the door behind her and the class.

"Daniel Boone Waggoner," I backed him against the wall and looked deep into his eyes. I wanted him to feel really uncomfortable. "Why did you tell your class I don't wear a shirt at home?" I demanded.

He kicked at the floor, "'Cause nobody else's mom does that."

"I don't do THAT either," I blurted out.

"But, Mom, they don't know it," Boone reasoned.

"No, dah! Well, Little Boone, they are going to know it because you are going to march right in there and tell them!" I hissed.

"But Mom, that will spoil everything. It will ruin my reputation. I just wanted them to think you are special, not normal like everyone else's mom," he whined.

"I don't care if it ruins your reputation because I am normal. This is a small town, Boone. If you want them to think I'm special, tell them I make super-duper chocolate chip cookies." I marched him to the door. "Now go in there and straighten this out!" I opened the door, shoved him through it, and closed it after him.

I fumed as Tandolynn and I clicked down the hall.

For the next few days, I racked my brain about what I could do to solve the problem. We live in a small town. I could put an ad in our once-a-week paper stating that the information 'little' Daniel Boone Waggoner shared in Show and Tell wasn't true. I crossed that idea out. Probably everybody who had not heard what he said would call to find out what he said. Besides, I hadn't told my husband yet. Actually, I hadn't decided if I wanted to tell him, and finally, I decided just to let the matter die.

Then, I noticed our Sunday school attendance boomed.

My husband was in seventh heaven.

I began to worry. Most of our visitors had kindergarten children. I stewed for about a month. At the end of our Sunday service, when my husband and I were shaking hands, Mr. Paulton, who owned the only legal tavern in our town, stepped in front of us. Beside him stood the little, tubby red-haired, blue-eyed girl from Boone's class. She reached up and tugged at my hand. "Mrs. Boone's Mom, I told my daddy it was only at home Boone said ya didn't wear nothin', but he wanted to check it out for his ownself."

I froze.

Scraps of Laughter
for Ladies

My husband's mouth dropped open.

Mr. Paulton scooped up his little red-haired, blue-eyed kindergarten girl, winked at me, and left, promising he would be back next Sunday.

In the silence that followed, my husband looked at me and raised his eyebrows about as far north as they would go.

"Later," I whispered....but we didn't have to wait for later. The head deacon, Mr. Banning, burst out laughing. Three other deacons joined until they were ready to roll on the floor.

"What is going on?" my husband demanded.

"You don't know?" Mr. Banning wiped tears from his eyes.

"Fill me in," my husband spoke with a deathly calm.

"Pastor, I can't believe you don't know. It's all over town. Why, we heard it at the coffee shop," Mr. Casey slapped his leg.

"What?" quietly, my husband asked.

"You know, about what Boone told his class in Show and Tell?" Mr. Clodfelter bellowed.

I thought I was going to die. A blank look crossed my husband's face as he shook his head.

Mr. Banning paused before he belted it out. "Boone told his class that your wife runs around the house with no clothes on."

"I do not! And Boone was supposed to tell those kids it wasn't true."

My husband turned to me. "You knew this?"

Scraps of Laughter
for Ladies

Weakly, I smiled.

My husband narrowed his eyes and studied me. "Well," he shook his head, "God works in mysterious ways. It seems this has brought in a whole new batch of souls that need the Lord. You know, if we put our heads together, we could come up with some very good things Boone could share in Show and Tell. That would bring them in. Why, we could get the whole town. We might even have to start a building program!"

I dropped my mouth and jabbed him in the ribs. The deacons grabbed their bellies with laughter... again.

As the weeks rolled by, I always made sure Boone had something for Show and Tell. When Friday came, we were in a hurry, and I hollered at Boone before he hit the door, "Show and Tell?"

He waved a jar in the air and shoved out the door.

"Oh," I thought. "Bugs. That's good. Kids always like jars of bugs." Without a care I started the laundry and progressed to the vacuuming.

The phone rang.

I switched off the sweeper and picked up the phone.

"Hello?"

"Mrs. Waggoner?"

My heart stopped. I would recognize that voice anywhere. It was Mrs. Garnell, Boone's teacher.

"Boone had something for Show and Tell, Mrs. Garnell, honest." I burst out.

Scraps of Laughter for Ladies

"Yes, yes, he did," she paused, "but I wonder if maybe you could screen 'little' Boone's Show and Tell a bit more carefully? When 'little' Boone pulled out his jar of dead warts and…"

"Dead warts?" I interrupted with a groan. "I thought he had bugs! Kids like bugs."

"Yes. Well, dead warts was the name 'little' Boone gave to the things in his jar, Mrs. Waggoner. Dead Warts. He said you had used something called Compound W and then dug them out with a machete one of your missionaries had given the church. Really, he was quite vivid and colorful in his description. Anyway, when he shoved the jar of dead warts under 'little' Amy Ridgewood's nose, she lost her lunch all over herself and three other little ones. And, I hesitate to say, but she is the principal's daughter. So, if you could better screen what 'little' Boone brings to Show and Tell, it would certainly help us."

"Yes, ma'am, Mrs. Garnell. Yes, ma'am, I surely will," I stuttered.

"Thank you, Mrs. Waggoner." She hung up.

"You're welcome, I'm sure," I told the empty receiver as I cradled it back on the phone. "Kindergarten," I groaned. "I still have 12 years of school to see him through…12 years…maybe more!"

When Boone walked in the door, he dropped his backpack while waving an envelope in the air. He be-lined straight to me past my husband. Beaming, he handed me the sealed envelope, "It's for you, mom, from the principal!"

Scraps of Laughter
for Ladies

My heart stopped.

My husband looked at me, "Anything I should know about, Dear?"

With wide eyes, I shrugged my shoulders. Slowly, I opened the note.

Dear Mrs. Waggoner,

Because of recent events, our school has unanimously decided to drop Show and Tell from our curriculum. We especially wanted to inform your household.

Sincerely,

Mr. Ridgewood, Principal (Amy's father)

"Yes!" I shouted.

"Shucks," Boone moaned. "It was my favorite subject!"

My husband shook his head. "And I was so looking forward to church growth and a new building program." He winked at me.

Scraps of Laughter for Ladies

The Best Lunch Ever!

My husband, Greg, is an evangelist. I love it. We meet the best people and watch the worst come to know Jesus Christ as their Savior. We travel coast to coast and see the beauty God has showered on America. We pop in on family, share a couple of days and sometimes only a few hours, until we part again.

In October, we were parked 40 minutes from Kansas City. We got a call from Greg's sister, Tricia, "You won't believe this, but I am in Kansas City babysitting my grandkids. Jenna is leaving me the car on Thursday, so do you want to meet for lunch?"

"Of Course!"

We set the time and place and counted the days until Thursday.

With excitement…plus…Greg always wants to be the first everywhere we go; we pulled into the parking lot early.

As we parked, his sister, Tricia, drove in. She was so busy looking for a parking place that she didn't see us. It seemed she wasn't even looking for us.

My husband laughed, "Don't say a word. I am going to get her good!"

Stealthy, he slipped from the pick-up, eased his door shut, and, on tiptoe, ran to the back of her car. Without sound, he bounded to the driver's door and plastered his backside against her window, holding her captive in the car while doing something like a back-and-forth line dance.

I had to see this! She was going to be so surprised. I jumped out of the truck and ran to watch from the front of her car. As reality hit, I gasped and threw my hand over my mouth. Ominous chills spread over my body. "Greg," I shouted, "Honey, that is not your sister!"

Greg frowned at me while continuing his window wiping with his backend, "You think I don't know my OWN sister?"

By now, the lady in the car, who was NOT his sister, was wildly flailing her hands. She grabbed her phone and began punching numbers. Her mouth hung wide, and her eyes bugged out.

"No! Honey, really, that is NOT your sister." I yelled.

Greg drew his black eyebrows together like when he preached about hellfire and damnation. He threw a pointing finger toward me, "Don't tell me that is not my sister. I know my own sister!"

I spread my hands, shrugged my shoulders, and mouthed to the lady in the car, "I am so sorry!"

Slowly, Greg absorbed my look. He slid down the window and turned to peek through the glass. His face drained of color. He held his hands wide and backed away from the car. In his loudest preaching voice, he explained, "I thought you were my sister. Ma'am, I am so sorry." He turned, shoved his hands in his pockets, and almost ran into the sandwich shop for hiding. After all, that was where we were going to meet his sister.

I found him sitting on a bench…alone and with his head in his hands.

I snuggled in beside him and whispered, "So, you know your OWN sister?" Then I exploded in laughter.

He glared.

Scraps of Laughter for Ladies

The lady from the car he had just sabotaged stepped into the sandwich shop, and I thought Greg was going to die. Again, he profusely apologized, explaining why he had committed such an act.

She laughed. She had calmed down quite a bit and took time to explain her feelings from her side of the story, "I thought you were a crazed, road-raged monster who I had cut off when I turned into the parking lot. I was so scared I couldn't remember the numbers to 911!"

We shared a laugh together.

Again, Greg apologized.

When Tricia arrived, we ordered, picked a table, and sat. Avoiding my husband's eyes, I spilled the story.

Finally, Greg was able to chuckle a bit.

When the waitress brought our order, we thanked her and then bowed for prayer. I cannot remember much of his prayer, but I know he ended with, "Thank you, Lord Mighty God, in heaven, for helping that lady to forget the number to 911!"

After the amen, we all laughed, and we shared the best lunch ever!

"A merry heart doeth good like a medicine…" Proverbs 22:17

Scraps of Laughter for Ladies

Baby Clay

One of the biggest surprises we ever had was Clay Charles, our third child. Oh, it wasn't that we did not want to have him; it was that we were not planning to have him. Our first two children, Daniel Boone and Tandolynn Laurel, we had prayed for. With God's help, we were blessed. Then, we hit the comfort zone. We had a boy and a girl…America's perfect family. We were done with getting up in the middle of the night, binkies, and potty training. Plus, Boone and Tandolynn were old enough that we could leave them with Nana and Papa or Grandma and Grandpa a few days at a time with no worries. I toyed with the idea of another baby, but there was no way I could ever convince Greg. The world had become too convenient. But…then God!

As always, it is a great shock when the comfort zone is busted open!

"What? How did that happen?" Greg wanted to know.

I just rolled my eyes.

Clay changed our life from the very first. We named him Clay because we were leaving it up to God to mold him. After all, it was God who had planned him.

We brought him home from the hospital, and I laid him on the ottoman while I went to the other room with the 'yuk' diaper I had just changed. When I came back, he was on the floor. I looked at Boone and Tandolynn, "How did Baby Clay get on the floor?"

Boone shrugged.

Scraps of Laughter
for Ladies

Tandolynn tipped her head and spread her hands, "I don't know."

I suspected…but to this day, I am not sure which one dropped him to the floor, but Baby Clay never let out a peep. I guess God had prepared him for older siblings.

When Baby Clay was about six months old and pretty well making all the baby sounds of goo-ing, gaga-ing, and blowing gurgle bubbles, we were sitting in the Blue Goose (the name of our car) while Daddy was filling up with fuel. Tandolynn tapped me on the shoulder and asked, "What is Baby Clay going to sound like when he starts talking?"

"Well, Honey," I began while watching her in the rear-view mirror. Answering kids' questions is like finding a path in the turbulent sea because you don't really know what they are asking. I smiled as I guessed what she was really asking. "I suppose he will sound just like you and Boone."

She leaned forward and put her hand to the side of her mouth to whisper, "But, Mama, what if he is Mexican, and we don't know it yet?"

I raised my eyebrows, blinked, and then I smiled, "Why don't you ask your daddy that question when he gets in the car?"

The minute her daddy slammed the car door shut, she asked him. "Daddy, what will Baby Clay sound like when he starts talking? I mean, what if he is Mexican, and we don't know it yet?"

He whipped his eyes to stare at Tandolynn in the rear-view mirror. "What?" Then he started laughing as he winked at me, "Baby Clay had better not be Mexican."

Scraps of Laughter
for Ladies

With three kids, my routine changed. I had no time. The minute Greg would walk through the door, I would shove Baby Clay into his arms, head to the bathroom, and lock the door. I wanted a bath…preferably a long bath, whether I needed it or not. Always I was interrupted by knocks on the door and little fingers slipping beneath and scratching the floor. And finally, Greg would come pounding, "Honey, Baby Clay needs you."

It seemed Baby Clay thought he needed me 24/7!

When the terrible twos hit, EVERYONE thought Baby Clay needed me. No one else would do.

One morning, Boone dragged Baby Clay to me, "Mom, Baby Clay got into my Legos, and I think he ate some of them. Can you get them out?"

I laughed, "Honey, God will get them out, but I don't know if you'll want them back."

"They are my Legos. Why would I not want them back?" Boone frowned.

Then, I described how God's process of getting them out of someone who ate them worked.

"Yuk!" Boone gagged. "He can keep them, but I'm shutting my door. Baby Clay can find somewhere else to sleep!"

"Sorry, Boone. You are brothers. You have to share a room."

Boone's shoulders sagged, but I found out later from his first-grade teacher that the 'Lego' experience was very educational. Boone shared the reclaiming of his Legos with vivid detail during show-and-tell. His teacher thought him to be very descriptive and, someday, maybe a great writer.

Scraps of Laughter
for Ladies

Baby Clay and Boone both inherited a big hunk from their dad. I call it the big 'fix-it slap'. When something is broken or just not working, Greg (and thus his sons) field try the fix with a slap to the side of the ailing thing, car, appliance, tire, T.V., or whatever stopped working. I don't know if the 'fix-it slap' ever really works. Maybe it jars things around, and some connection reconnects, but nine times out of ten, I would say it helps the male frustration more than anything that needs to be fixed. But as a target shooting device? I don't think you could market it.

Greg and I were sitting at the dining room table after lunch. He needed to make a phone call, and in the parsonage, we had a landline. He reached around and grabbed it from the breakfast bar, picked up the receiver, and dialed the number. Nothing happened. He clicked the hang-up button several times and tried it again. Still nothing. He pulled the phone from his ear and studied the receiver. Again, he put it to his ear. Nothing. He tightened his lips into a grim line, furrowed his brows, and whopped the side of the phone with his 'fix-it slap'.

I jumped. You would think I would be used to this by now. "Honey?" I interrupted the silence, "Do you really think that will make the phone work? And what if your 'fix it slap' breaks it?"

"The phone doesn't work, so if it breaks, what have we got to lose?"

Baby Clay giggled.

I looked at him, rolled my eyes, and took a deep breath. "Your 'fix-it' slap is not going to fix the phone, Honey."

"What?" Greg narrowed his eyes. "Why not?" he asked.

Scraps of Laughter for Ladies

I pointed to Clay. He sat holding a pair of scissors, the tool he had chosen this time. The phone wire had been snipped into one-inch sections all the way from the floor to the phone.

I smiled and asked, "So, did the whopping of the phone work this time?"

"No, but the whipping of a boy might." He leaned over and scooped up his son, "And where did you get a pair of scissors, Young Man?"

Clay giggled and repeated the word, "Scickers. Boone, scickers."

Boone and Tandolynn had to learn. If you don't want your little brother to get it…put it where he can't reach it.

Greg loves his tools, too. So do his sons. Of the many tools, Clay's favorite through the terrible twos seemed to be markers, especially permanent black ones. For a while, we called him Marker Man. He left his mark on books, walls, and furniture. We had an antique white settee, which he turned into a pen stripe.

One afternoon, I was working in the kitchen. I kept hearing a patterned pounding, and I decided I had better search it out. I found Clay with a gallon jar full of caterpillars. The season had been abundantly filled with the furry creatures. Boone and Tandolynn had caught over 100 of them and stashed them in an old pickle jar. Then Boone hammered holes in the lid so the busy, little critters could breathe.

I watched as Clay opened the lid, pulled out a furry beast, laid it on the floor, carefully closed the lid so the rest of the caterpillars couldn't escape, picked up the hammer, and smashed the caterpillar. I sighed. Yep. He liked tools just like his father.

Scraps of Laughter
for Ladies

I went to the back door and called, "Boone! Tandolynn! If you want these caterpillars, you had better come to rescue them from your brother… and the sooner, the better!"

The two came crashing through the door and stopped in horror as they watched Baby Clay. Tandolynn gasped. Boone sort of smiled and snickered as though he thought it looked like fun, and he might join in.

Tandolynn bee-lined to her brother, yanked the hammer from his hand, and scolded him. Baby Clay squalled. Just like his father, he didn't like his tools taken away from him.

Tandolynn marched to my very rounded tummy and poked me with her pointing finger, "I hate brothers. And I'll tell you what. This had better not be another brother!"

As I looked into my daughter's wild eyes, I thought, "Dear Lord, you are going to have to save Clay from his sister so you will have a chance to mold him."

Lucky Tandolynn. It wasn't another brother. Kelloway Dee was born just before our family was uprooted. We took a pastorate in Amarillo, Texas. Gone were the country days as we were dumped into city life. Traffic, horns, sirens, gunshots, and fights stole our freedom. I kept the kids caged in the backyard. But we were blessed. Thompson Park was just across the freeway from our home, and when we wanted to escape city life, I would gather the kids and an old, stale bag of bread. We loaded up in the van and headed for Thompson Park to feed the ducks on the lake. It was really a big pond, but everyone in the city called it a lake. Since Clay had just had his third

Scraps of Laughter
for Ladies

birthday, he got to hold the bread bag. I stopped the van. The kids poured out the doors and ran toward the water.

Thompson Park ducks were not afraid of people. They had been fed so often that they expected people to bring food for them. When the kids headed their way, the ducks put their scrawny legs in high gear with necks stretched out, wings flapping, and beaks wide open, hissing and honking. Clay's eyes nearly jumped out of his head. He froze for what seemed like eons, then sprang into action. The only weapon he had was the bread sack. He took hold with both hands and began swinging and whopping the ducks over their heads. A fighting frenzy floundered closer. Feathers and breadcrumbs filled the air and littered the grass. Boone rammed into the fray, frantically kicking the frightened birds from his brother. Tandolynn shoved through the fury, grabbed Clay, and pulled him to safety. When they reached the comfort of Mama, Clay took a death grip on my leg. He was shaking. I pulled him up with one arm as I held Baby Kelloway in the other. I smiled and blew a feather from his soft hair. "So...are you done feeding the ducks?" I asked.

Baby Clay nodded. There were no tears, but fear shot from his eyes.

During Clay's little boy years, he donned a Superhero suit made from his blue Superman pajamas with a pair of red skivvies over the top of them. He jumped, ran, and performed Superhero tricks throughout the neighborhood with his cape flying behind. He wore them 24/7... if I let him. I made him change for church services, and it broke his heart if I took them to launder. I think he was afraid I might wash the 'super' out of his hero suit. I smile as I remember his high school years. It worked out that his school colors were blue and red, and that Clay had become the fastest runner on the track team. The Amarillo Globe News dubbed him 'Superman'.

What sweet memories.

Baby Clay is no longer Baby Clay, but the talents and gifts God chose to bless him with continue to amaze Greg and me. He works with metal and wood and draws wonderfully. I would have to say one of the best things he has brought into this world is our granddaughter, Kelli. I am proud to say she takes after her daddy, Baby Clay. What a surprise he was, and Greg and I have thanked God for that surprise package over and over again.

Scraps of Laughter
for Ladies

The Christmas Program

Kelloway, be sure you bring the mashed potatoes when you come so we can put them in the church warmer.

"Okay, Mom, but just for the record, I still think it is wrong."

Clay laughed, "Mashed potatoes? There is nothing wrong with mashed potatoes."

"No," Kelloway glared, "I am talking about using a real baby for baby Jesus."

"I am glad we are. I think it's cool. The dead doll thing is old," Clay told her.

"Really?" Kelloway raised her eyebrows, "We are using Kelli's baby sister, Emma, so what do you think of that?"

Clay shrugged, "A girl? For Baby Jesus? Who's going to know? All babies look alike and sound alike and stink alike."

Kelloway held her finger in the air with foreboding, "But we are talking about baby Jesus, and I don't think he should be a she. That is just wrong."

I smiled, "It is just a Christmas program, Kelloway, and again, no one will know. The Braumbaucks offered us the use of their baby because her sister, Kelli is Mary, and her brother, Buster is Joseph. It was very nice of them, so I accepted."

"But, Mom, they are bus kids, and their mom and dad don't even come to church," Kelloway spread her hands.

"But they will come for this, and maybe, just maybe, they will hear the Word, and it will change their lives forever."

213

Scraps of Laughter
for Ladies

"Maybe? That is a lot of maybes," Kelloway shook her head.

I turned to pick up the Walmart sack with a ham, threw an old bathrobe over my shoulder for a shepherd costume, and stuck a foil crown on my head for one of the three kings. As I stepped out the door, I called, "Clay, don't eat any more of those cookies. They are for church dinner. Be sure you bring them all when you come."

I closed the door and rapidly walked over the porch and down the steps. I noticed it must have been misting. The driveway was wet. I probably should have a coat, but there was no way I was going back for one. I took about three steps and discovered the mist had frozen into black ice. My Sunday heels skidded and slid, and I slapped down on my buns. I spun in a complete circle while sliding down the drive toward the street. I grabbed at something, anything, even air to stop. Finally, the gutter came to my rescue. I sat all sprawled in that gutter, my velvet dress hiked over my chubby knees and the foil crown dangling from my glasses. Quickly, I looked to see if anyone had watched my Wide World of Sports' agony of defeat. "Thank you, Lord," I whispered. No one was in sight.

I still clutched my old bathrobe and an empty, busted Walmart bag. My ham was gone. I had to have that ham. DeeDee was doing the turkey, but alone, it would not be enough for our Church Christmas dinner. I rolled over and out of the gutter to my hands and knees. I tried crawling back over my runway. Slipping and sliding halfway up the drive, I spotted the ham smack dab under the old Ford pick-up. I groaned. I had to belly crawl to reach it. Just as I retrieved my prize and pulled out from under the truck, the Browns drove

214

Scraps of Laughter
for Ladies

by. The kids pointed and waved, but I don't think their mom and dad saw me. I hoped. "Thank you, Lord," again I whispered.

Crawling, I dragged my prize up the driveway and waited to pull myself to my feet on the grass where I had decided to walk the rest of the way to the church. My dress was not in the best shape, but it would have to do. There was no time to change if I was to get this ham cooked before Christmas Dinner. Luckily, it would be dark in the sanctuary for the program, and I would wear an apron in the kitchen, which I would 'forget to take off' throughout dinner. Voila! The front of my dress was covered!

I was a little sore, but after the program and dinner I would go home and lay on the heating pad. I could make it. I knew I could.

Our platform is perfect for children's programs. Seven long steps up seat our children's choir. We moved the podium, which makes a great square for the manger scene, and the other side of the platform was set apart for the puppets to perform.

I was watching the puppets when, out of the corner of my eye, I saw a problem developing in the choir. On the very top row, the angels were lined up. Beneath them, the shepherds and the wise men stood. Colt was a squat shepherd with freckles sprinkled over his face. Colt was an activist for trouble. He could talk anyone into anything, and he had been talking. The shepherd beside him was Jermy: short for Jeremy, but everyone called him Jermy. The name fit him better, and he was used to it. I watched Colt nudge him and nod a 'go-a-head.' Jermy twitched a bit, then he took his staff, hooked it onto Marianne's halo, and lifted. Marianne had her halo pinned on tight, so when Jermy

215

Scraps of Laughter
for Ladies

pushed harder, her face scrunched up in pain. Her hands left the prayerful pose and balled into fists. War was about to begin.

I had to intervene.

The lights were on the puppets, not the choir, so I quietly crossed and climbed the steps to unwind the staff from the halo. I needed to hurry because there were only a few more lines from the puppets before the lights would dim on them and come up on the choir. I took the steps two at a time. After I got the staff untangled from Marianne's halo, I decided I needed to give a warning to Colt and Jermy to quit messing with Marianne's or anyone else's halo. Then, I could scuttle back to my place. However, Marianne whipped around and hit me right in the face with her wing. That wing knocked me off balance, and I stepped backward. There was no step…only air. I cascaded down, catching a couple of Christmas carolers in my path. They squealed as they tumbled with me. Just as we landed, the lights were directed to the choir. Madly, I crawled to the front pew through a volley of gasps. I could only hope the audience had seen the two little choir members and not me. Our light man was on his toes. He flipped the lights off, shrouding all in darkness, which made the kids fidgety, and I crawled smack into the pew, whacking my head, which echoed through the whole sanctuary. Again, the audience drew in their breath, and I heard someone say, "That was the Preacher's wife. I am sure of it."

So much for secrecy!

The lights flipped on the choir. The two Christmas Carolers who had fallen with me were now huddled together on the floor beside me. I let them stay there. With one hand, I rubbed my head, and with the

other, I led the choir in the song, 'We Three Kings.'
The three kings slipped from the group with their gifts
and journeyed around the auditorium and up the steps
to the manger scene. Two shepherds stood while the
first shepherd knelt low to place his gift before the
manger. As he rose, I could hear Mary whisper, "You
bum, you are supposed to leave the treasure chest for
the King of Kings."

"I can't. It is stuck," he wailed back.

"You want to bet?" Mary grabbed the treasure
chest and yanked. I guess the wise man had forgotten
what he brought, opened the chest earlier to peek in,
and shut it. Only he had clamped it tight on his beard.
When Mary grabbed the treasure chest and jerked, the
wise man's beard held on with a sturdy strip of elastic
pulled away from his face. Mary unlatched the chest,
and the beard popped the wise man in the mouth. He
yelped in pain.

Baby Jesus woke up and squalled.

Mary shook her finger at the wise man and
scolded, "Now see what you have done. You woke up
Baby Jesus! Set this treasure where it goes, and you
can leave," she ordered and handed him the chest.

Baby Jesus howled.

Mary grabbed the swaddled baby from the
manger and scolded, "Hush it up right now, Emma."
Then she whopped Baby Jesus on the buns.

The audience sucked in their breath. I just quit
breathing. My husband, the Pastor, was rolling in silent
laughter on the front row.

After our last song, I gathered all our kids in the
front rows to listen to my husband's Christmas
devotion. The kids wiggled and snickered and finally
settled to listen.

Scraps of Laughter
for Ladies

My husband, the Pastor, began, "I remember growing up, running into the house, and almost never shutting the door. Always my mom or dad would call, 'Son, were you born in a barn?'"

Everyone in the auditorium laughed.

My husband let the laughter settle before he continued. "Yes, Baby Jesus was born in a barn, but he opened a door that no one can ever shut. He was the Lamb of God. It was fitting that Jesus should be born in a barn. He is our lamb, our sacrifice for our sins. He was nailed on the cross, and there he spent his last breath for us. But…Jesus did not stay dead. Yes, he was our sacrifice, but he conquered death and rose to be our Saviour: from sacrifice to Saviour, what a miracle! Psalms 85:10 reads, 'Mercy and truth are met together; righteousness and peace have kissed each other.' Mercy: the Lamb of God was our sacrifice. That is mercy! Truth: because of our sins, we must have a sacrifice. Jesus was and is without sin. Righteousness: the Lamb of God was the only one righteous enough to be our sacrifice. And peace? Peace: will only come when the Lamb of God has become your sacrifice and your Saviour. That door Jesus opened by being born the Lamb of God in a stable, to dying on the cross and rising as Saviour is still open for you. If anyone would like to walk through that door and invite Jesus to be your Saviour, please come." Softly, music sifted over the crowd, and together, the Braumbaucks stepped into the aisle heading toward that open door.

My heart sputtered, beating the happiest rhythm as it sang to the Lord, "Truly, Lord, you can use anything. Thank you for using our messed-up children's program."

Scraps of Laughter for Ladies

When the final song was sung, I sighed in relief. My husband thanked everyone, and they clapped like they never had before. I found that in make-believe and in God's house, all is forgiven…but never forgotten. The dinner went well…it was a very tender ham. I think it had been beaten to death under the old blue pick-up. And believe me, when I got home, I put on a well-worn bathrobe, latched onto the couch with the heating pad, rubbed my temples, and breathed, "Yes, that is over for another year! And thank you, Lord, for the blessings!"

Kelloway swung the door open and laughed, "So no one will know Baby Jesus is a girl, right, Mom?"

Before I could ground that child of mine, my husband came bouncing in, winked, and said, "Nice program, dear! I had a lot of comments. I told everyone to e-mail them to you as you would like to respond personally."

"You did not!" I wailed. I could imagine all the comments. I did not want them and surely did not want to respond to them.

But before he could answer, my phone dinged.